Praise for *You Know Me Well*

"*You Know Me Well* perfectly encapsulates those fraught, end-all-be-all feelings of high-school romance and graduation. . . . The raw emotion of this novel will delight fans of Rainbow Rowell and John Green." —*BookPage*

"Both authors excel at writing smart, funny, and realistic dialogue. These are characters to whom readers will relate and want to get to know." —*School Library Journal*

"Incisively explore[s] the excitement and costs of change, and the importance of friends in figuring out what to keep and what to jettison." —*Publishers Weekly*

"The pacing and voices of LaCour's and Levithan's alternating points of view are on point, keeping this sweet . . . tale moving gladly forward." —*Kirkus Reviews*

"Often subtle and always absorbing examination of fraught relationships . . . Popular authors LaCour and Levithan tell their heartfelt story seamlessly in chapters that alternate between Mark's and Kate's respective points of view and invite readers' emotional engagement with these two empathetic teens." —*Booklist*

"LaCour and Levithan join together to give an honest view of the anxious teenage psyche. A perfect read for the bolter in all of us." —*RT Book Reviews*

"Teens, queer or straight, are often dramatic and unsure of themselves, and by moving its characters beyond the coming-out trope and giving them other questions to focus on, this book gives them room to be." —*The Horn Book*

"LaCour and Levithan are both dab hands at utopian romance." —*The Bulletin of the Center for Children's Books*

"Nina LaCour and David Levithan are two of the best YA authors working right now, and this story is further proof. . . . This fun, sweet novel beautifully captures the power of romantic and platonic love alike." —*Seventeen* magazine
(Top 10 YA Books of 2016)

"Few literary titles have been able to portray adult romance as honestly and believably as LaCour and Levithan manage to in this irresistible teenage tale. I can only hope this isn't the last we hear from Kate and Mark." —EDGE Media Network

"Levithan and LaCour beautifully capture what it's like to have a romance against the backdrop of the cool gray city of love. There is something about this place that renders everything full of magic." —*Forever Young Adult*

"A sweet, hopeful story about finding the courage to live your truth—whatever it may be. And of course, it's a story about the friends who guide us through it all." —*Bustle*
(Beach Reads for Summer 2016)

"This is the story of two people who didn't realize how badly they needed someone until they found each other. And after spending a wild, heartbreaking, magical week with them in San Francisco, readers will feel lucky this book managed to find them as well. I know I do." —Jennifer E. Smith,
author of *Hello, Goodbye, and Everything in Between*

you know me well

A NOVEL

**NINA LaCOUR
& DAVID LEVITHAN**

St. Martin's Griffin New York

YOU KNOW ME WELL. Copyright © 2016 by Nina LaCour and David Levithan. All rights reserved. Printed in the United States of America. For information, address St. Martin's Press, 175 Fifth Avenue, New York, N.Y. 10010.

www.stmartins.com

Designed by Meryl Sussman Levavi

The Library of Congress has cataloged the hardcover edition as follows:

Names: LaCour, Nina, author. | Levithan, David, author.
Title: You know me well / Nina LaCour and David Levithan.
Description: First edition. | New York : St. Martin's Griffin, 2016.
Identifiers: LCCN 2016001129 | ISBN 9781250098641 (hardcover) | ISBN 9781250098665 (e-book)
Subjects: | CYAC: Love—Fiction. | Friendship—Fiction. | Homosexuality—Fiction. | BISAC: JUVENILE FICTION / Love & Romance. | JUVENILE FICTION / Social Issues / Friendship.
Classification: LCC PZ7.L13577 You 2016 | DDC [Fic]—dc23
LC record available at https://lccn.loc.gov/2016001129

ISBN 978-1-250-09865-8 (trade paperback)

Our books may be purchased in bulk for promotional, educational, or business use. Please contact your local bookseller or the Macmillan Corporate and Premium Sales Department at 1-800-221-7945, extension 5442, or by e-mail at MacmillanSpecialMarkets@macmillan.com.

First St. Martin's Griffin Trade Paperback Edition: June 2017

10 9 8 7 6 5 4

To Kristyn
(of course)
—N

To Billy, Nick, and Zack
(for Big Gay Lunch and everything else)
—D

SATURDAY

MARK

1

Right now, my parents think I'm sleeping on the couch at my best friend Ryan's house, safely tucked into a suburban silence. At the same time, Ryan's parents think he's in the top bunk in my bedroom, slumbering peacefully after a slow night of video games and TV. In reality, we're in the Castro, at a club called Happy Happy, kicking it up at the gaygantuan kickoff party for San Francisco's very own Pride Week. The whole spectrum is in attendance tonight, breathing in the rainbow air and dancing to the rainbow sounds. Ryan and I are underage, underexperienced, underdressed, and completely under the spell of the scene pressing up against us. Ryan looks a little bit scared, but he's trying to hide it under an arched brow and a smoke screen of sarcasm. If someone he doesn't like approaches us, he'll hold my hand to make himself seem taken, but otherwise it's hands-off. In the context of our relationship, this counts as logic: We are just friends except for the moments when, oops, we're more than just friends. We don't talk about these moments, and I think Ryan believes if we don't talk about them, then they haven't been happening. That's what he wants.

I don't know what I want, so mostly I go along.

It was my idea to come here, but I never would have been able to do it without Ryan at my side. I've stuck to the halls of our high school, living my out-to-everyone life pretty much the same as before everyone (including me) knew. Only now it's the last week of junior year, and it felt like it was time to take that forty-five-minute leap into the city. "Sweet sixteen and never been risked," Ryan calls my life—as if he's been sneaking out any more than I have. Luckily, I look older than I am—to the point that an opposing coach once wanted to see my records, to make sure I wasn't a college-age ringer. I don't have a fake ID or anything, but at a place like Happy Happy on the first night of Pride, it's not like they check. We just had to look like we knew what we were doing, and that got us in.

I was a little surprised when Ryan said he'd come, because he insists that his being gay is "nobody's business." Where this leaves me I'm not exactly sure. There are times I want to shake him and say, Dude, I'm the baseball player with the jock friends and you're the sensitive poet who edits the lit mag—shouldn't *I* be the one who's scared? But then I think I'm not being nice, or at least not being understanding, since Ryan has to figure things out for himself. There is no way whatsoever to figure things out for someone else. Even if he's your best friend who you always end up fooling around with.

It's really dark and there isn't much room to move. We're getting plenty of wolfish looks from other guys. When they're cute, I think Ryan likes it. But I feel awkward. Meeting someone new was not the reason I came here, although maybe it crossed Ryan's mind when he said yes. There are some guys at the party who look like what my dad would look like if he wore lots of leather, and there are others who look like they're auditioning for selfies. Everyone's sentences crash together to make this gigantic noise, and my thoughts overlap so much that all I can feel is their loudness.

The parties I've gone to before have been held in basements and school gyms. Now it's like I've walked into a wider, narrower world. Robyn is singing about dancing on her own, and people are verbing their bodies along to that. These are not the people I usually hang with. We are not in Brewster's rec room, watching a Giants game. This is not a beer crowd. Everyone here is a cocktail.

We're not quite at the bar and not quite on the dance floor. Ryan's about to say something, but a man with a camera interrupts by leaning in front of him and asking me who I am. He can't be older than thirty, but he has bright silver hair.

"Excuse me?" I shout over the noise.

"Who are you?" he asks again.

"I'm Mark," I say. "Why?"

"Do you model?"

Ryan snickers at this.

"No!" I answer.

"You should!" the guy says.

I'm thinking he can't be serious, but he takes out his card and gives it to me. Before I can say anything else, there's the pop-burst of a flash. I'm still blinking in the afterglow when the photographer touches my wrist and tells me to email him. Then he vanishes back into the crowd.

"What was *that*?" I ask Ryan.

"Are you talking to me?" he replies. "I'm afraid I'm currently invisible. Or at least I'm invisible to noted fashion photographers."

Ryan is just as cute as I am, but it's against the rules for me to tell him that.

I let the card drop to the floor and say, "Whatever."

Ryan bends down, picks it up, and hands it back.

"Keep it as a souvenir," he tells me. "I mean, it's not like you're actually going to do anything about it."

"Who says?"

"Let's just say history is on my side."

Not untrue. I am shy. Sometimes painfully shy. And it's especially painful when someone reminds me about it.

"Can we look around some more?" I ask. "Maybe dance a little?"

"You know I don't dance."

What he means is: He doesn't dance when other people are watching. This was his excuse when I wanted to go to our junior prom together. It would have been a big step for us, and he looked at me like I'd asked if he wanted to make out in a shark tank. In front of his parents. Instead of saying we couldn't go to the prom because he wanted to keep us a secret, he wrapped his refusal in a blanket dismissal of dancing. I knew he wasn't going to put me through the indignity of watching him go with someone else—he wasn't going to try to live *that* lie, at least. But he wasn't going to go with me, either.

I ended up staying home instead. He came over and I

thought he was going to make it up to me, but instead we watched *There Will Be Blood*. Then he went home.

I can understand not wanting to dance in front of everyone we know. I can see that's a big deal. But I was hoping it would be different here. I was hoping that being among all these happy, happy strangers would change the game.

"C'mon," I say, trying to keep my tone light. "It's Pride Week!"

Ryan's eye has already moved elsewhere. I follow his gaze to find this very pretty college guy in Clark Kent glasses and a simple blue T-shirt with a slight rip on the left shoulder. He'd be the apple of any bookworm's eye—he's much more Ryan's type than I'll ever be. He senses Ryan looking at him . . . then senses me looking at him and meets my eye instead of Ryan's. I quickly look away.

"I saw him first," Ryan mutters. I think he might be joking, but something in the pit of my stomach tells me he's not. Then he says, "Oh *man*." I look back up, and Indie Bookstore Clark Kent has his arms around a boy who's wearing a ski hat even though it's June. Hat Boy leans in for a kiss and Clark gleefully obliges. If it were manga, hearts would be rising like balloons over their heads.

"Happy Happy is depressing depressing me," Ryan says. "You promised me fun. Where's the fun?"

That had been my big argument—*it'll be fun*. What I didn't add was that I thought the idea of sneaking out of my house, tiptoeing to the train, and coming into the city where no one else really knows us would be . . . romantic, I guess. On the ride in, it was almost like that, like it was an adventure we were sharing. I pressed my leg against his and he didn't move away. We sat there making jokes and imagining the look on my mother's face if she checked up on us and found the room empty. (My mother gets upset when a pillow is out of place on the sofa.) I thought that people looking at us would see a couple, and I got a sense of confirmation from that.

Now I'm guessing we look like two friends. I probably look like Ryan's wingman.

"I want a drink," he declares.

"You'll get caught," I remind him.

"No, I won't. Have some faith. Some of us aren't Timid Timmys."

I follow him as he presses into the crowd and makes his way to the bar. I wonder what would happen if I stopped walking, if I let the crowd fill up the space between us. Would he notice? Would he wade back to find me? Or would he keep going, because forward is his destination and I am not?

I falter for a moment, and in that moment he reaches for my hand. As if he senses my doubts. As if he doesn't need to turn around to know exactly where I am. As if everything we've been through has at least constructed this connection, this much of a bridge.

"Stay with me," he says.

So I do. And when we get to the bar, Charming Ryan returns. The shadows fall from his mood. When the bartender comes over, Ryan tosses out his words like he knows they'll float into the ears of anyone who hears them. The bartender smiles; he can't help but like Ryan. This is the boy I fell for, about eight years after we first became friends. This is the boy who made me want to be who I am. This is the boy I can borrow my confidence from.

The bartender comes back with two flutes of champagne,

and I can't help but laugh at how silly it is. Even though I don't drink, Ryan slides one of the glasses over to me.

"Just one sip," he says. "If you don't, it won't be a toast. It'll just be a burnt piece of bread."

I relent and raise my glass. We clink, and then I sip while he downs. When he's done, I give him mine to finish off.

"I wish you'd live a little," he says when the bubbly's been popped.

"What does that mean?" I ask, even though we've had this conversation before.

"Nothing."

"It's not nothing."

"No, it is. It's precisely nothing."

"What's precisely nothing?"

"The degree to which you put yourself out there."

I have no idea why this has become the subject.

"What are you talking about? A failure to finish my champagne makes me—what? A Cowardly Connor?"

"It's not just that." He points his empty glass at the crowd. "This room is full of attractive men. You are a fine specimen of boyness. But you're not even looking around. You're not trying. That guy gave you a card you'll never use. Other guys keep looking at you. You could totally work it. But you don't want to."

"What would you have me do?" I spy the sign-up sheet next to his elbow. "Join the midnight underwear contest? Dance around on the bar?"

"Yes! That is *exactly* what I'd have you do!"

"So I can find a guy to hook up with?"

"Or *talk to*. Don't look at me that way—we're far from the

only teenagers in this place. Mr. Right could be right here, right now."

Can't you see it's you? the part of me that should know better wants to ask. But that, too, is against the rules.

"Fine," I say, and before Ryan can say another word I am reaching across the bar for the clipboard. I pull the ever-present pen from his pocket and write my name down.

Ryan laughs. "No way. There's no way you'll follow through on that."

"Watch me," I say—even though I know he's right. I'm fine in the locker room, or with Ryan. But in public? In my underwear? That would seem about as likely as me going home with a girl.

Still, it's one thing for me to have it in my head that I'm not going to do it and quite another for Ryan to have it in *his* head. Because the more he insists I'm going to flake out, the more I want to prove him wrong. There's definitely a double standard here—there's no way he would do it, either. But I'm the one who's being dared.

We bicker along these lines for a few more minutes, and then it's midnight and the DJ is telling all the underwear contestants to make their way to the bar. The bartender puts all the names in an upturned pink wig, then yells my name out first, followed by nine others. The man next to me immediately starts to take off his clothes, exposing a steel-armor chest and graph-paper abs. I think I may have seen him swimming in the Olympics, or maybe it's his Speedo-shaped underwear that's tricking me. The bartender says we'll be starting in a minute.

"Now or never," Ryan tells me. From the way he says it, I can tell his money's on never.

I kick off my shoes. As Ryan watches, dumbstruck, I pull off my jeans, then remove my socks, because leaving my socks on would look ridiculous. I cannot give myself any time to think about what I'm doing. It feels strange to be standing barefoot in the middle of a packed club. The floor is sticky. I pull my shirt over my head.

I am in my underwear. Surrounded by strangers. I thought I'd be cold, but instead it's like I'm feeling the heat of the club more fully. All these bodies clouding the air. And me, right at the center of it.

I don't think I'd recognize myself, and that's okay.

The bartender calls out my name. I hand my shirt to Ryan and jump onto the bar.

My heart is pounding so hard I can hear it in my ears.

There are loud cheers, and the DJ throws Rihanna's "Umbrella" into the speakers. I have no idea what I'm supposed to do. I am standing on a bar in my red-and-blue boxer briefs, afraid I'll knock over people's drinks. Obligingly, the patrons pull their glasses down, and before I know what I'm doing I'm . . . moving. I'm pretending I'm in my bedroom, dancing around in my underwear, because that is certainly something I do often enough. Just not with an audience. Not with people hooting and whistling. I am swiveling my hips and I am raising my hand in the air and I am singing along with the "-ella, -ella, -eh, -eh-." Most of all I am looking at the expression on Ryan's face, which is one of pure astonishment. I have never seen his smile so wide or so bright. I have never felt him so proud of me. He is whooping at the top of his lungs. I point at him and match his smile with my own. I dance with him, even though he's down there and I'm up here. I let everybody see how much I love him and he doesn't shy away from it, because for a moment he's not thinking about that—he's only thinking about me.

I take it all in. The world, from this vantage point, is crazy-beautiful. I look around the crowd and see all these people enjoying themselves—having fun with me or making fun of me or imagining having fun with me. Pairs of guys and pairs of women. Young skateboarders and men who look like bank presidents on their day off. People from all over the Bay Area patchwork, many of them dancing along, some of them starting to throw money my way. Clark Kent's in the crowd, looking me over. When I see him, I swear he winks.

I feel my gaze pulling itself back to Ryan. I feel myself coming back to him. But along the way, someone else catches my eye. Before I can return to Ryan—while I'm still up there in my underwear, thinking he's the only person in this whole place who knows who I am—I see another face I know. It's like the song stops for a second, and I'm thrown. Because, yes, it has to be her. Here, in this gay bar, watching me dance near naked over a carpet of dollar bills.

Katie Cleary.

The senior I sit next to in Calculus.

Kate

2

"Tell me about her again," I say.

I change lanes on the top deck of the Bay Bridge so that we get the best view of the city lights, even though June and Uma are kissing in the backseat, oblivious to the scenery, and Lehna is busy scrolling through her phone for the next song we should listen to.

She laughs. "I don't know if there's anything left to tell."

"It's okay if I've heard it before."

The first chords of "Divided" by Tegan and Sara start to play, and for a moment I remember what it felt like for Lehna and me to stand in the sea of girl-loving girls at their concert when we were in eighth grade, how I felt something deep in the core of my heart and my stomach that told me *yes*.

"She got home on Tuesday," Lehna says. "And she was pretty

jet-lagged, but she told me she was used to traveling, not getting much sleep, keeping weird hours in general. When I talked to her on the phone she was sewing sequins onto a scarf. She says she likes to sparkle at Pride."

"Do I look too plain tonight? I am the opposite of sparkling."

I began worrying about what to wear several weeks ago, but that didn't make me any closer to a solution by the time today got here. I ended up choosing what I hoped would look a little bohemian, effortless but still put together. A soft, light chambray button-up tucked into darker jeans. A brown belt with a turquoise buckle. High-heeled boots. Long, diamond-shaped bronze earrings and bright red lipstick. I put my hair into a loose side braid that falls over my shoulder. In between moments of almost-paralyzing self-doubt, I looked in the mirror and thought, for about half a second, that I looked like the kind of person I might like to know if I didn't know myself already.

"You look great!" June calls from the backseat.

"I would totally fall in love with you," Uma says.

Lehna says, "Yeah. You look European, which Violet will appreciate. And after the performers she's been hanging out with, you'll probably seem refreshingly normal."

That word—*normal*—it fills me with panic.

"Make sure to remember to reapply your lipstick. It brings out the green in your eyes."

I nod. I will. I turn up the music and try to calm myself down. Out the window, the lights of the city spread before us, full of so much promise. People in the cars around us are smiling or nodding their heads to music. We are all on our way to the same party even if it's taking place in hundreds of different bars and living rooms. We are going out to celebrate ourselves and one another. To fall in love or to remind ourselves of all the people we've loved in the past. For me that would be a very short list. Which is part of why tonight scares me so much.

Lehna and I have been friends since we were six, so I've known about her cousin Violet for years. The daughter of Lehna's photojournalist aunt, Violet has never lived in one place for more than a year, has never attended a traditional school, and has been traveling across Europe for the past twenty months, studying with trapeze artists while her mother documents circus life. Violet's always been a source of fascination. Even more so when, last year, she wrote to Lehna from Prague and told her she'd fallen in love with a girl. Violet described it in a way that no one living a normal life in a California suburb could explain it. She used words like *passionate* and phrases like *love affair*. The girl was from the Swiss Alps and her name was Mathilde and it began and ended over the span of two weeks, from the moment the circus got to town to the moment it packed up and left.

And then, a couple months later, Violet wrote again to say that she was going to move back to San Francisco. Her mother was continuing the circus project, but Violet was turning eighteen and wanted to make her own life. *I want to know how it feels to stay in one place for a little while,* she wrote. *So I'm coming home, even though I don't even remember what the seasons feel like there.* When Lehna exclaimed late one night that she should set Violet and me up, I pretended that the thought hadn't occurred to me, when really it was all I'd been thinking about for months.

"Remember to call me Kate in front of her," I say.

"Got it. Kate-not-Katie."

"Thanks," I say, even though I can tell by her smirk and the tone of her voice that she's annoyed.

I exit onto Duboce. I've driven us to this house a few times. It's a classic San Francisco Victorian with small rooms and high ceilings. Lehna's friend Shelbie lives there along with a big chocolate Lab and parents who never seem to be home. Violet knows her, too. Shelbie's mom and Lehna's mom and aunt go way back, I guess. I don't totally understand the connection, but I am willing to accept it because it's taking me a step closer to finally meeting Violet.

Now that we are actually in the city, my dad's old Jeep taking us closer and closer to where we're going, the streets full of celebrating people, the night buzzing all around us, I feel my hands start to shake.

I know that it's just a first meeting. I know that Violet has already heard about me and that she wants to meet me, too. I know that it shouldn't be the end of the world if it doesn't work out between us. But the embarrassing truth is that I have far too much at stake to be casual about this.

When I'm sitting through History, listening to my teacher drone on about dates and the names of battles, I think about Violet. At night, as I do the dinner dishes listening to love songs through oversize headphones, I think about Violet. I think about her when I wake up in the morning and when I'm mixing oil paints and when I'm getting books out of my locker. And when I begin to worry that I chose the wrong college, or that my future roommate will hate me, or that I'm going to grow up and forget about the things I once loved— cobalt blue, this certain hill behind my high school, searching for old slides at flea markets, the song "Divided"—I think about Violet. She's swinging from a trapeze, mending colorful costumes, driving in a caravan across Europe while cracking jokes with fire-breathers and tightrope walkers—then coming home to San Francisco and falling in love with me.

"There's something I should mention," Lehna says as we make our way down Guerrero Street. "I may have told her you had a solo show coming up at a gallery in the city."

"*What?*"

"We were talking about how good of a painter you are, and then I just got carried away for a second."

"But I don't even *know* any galleries in the city," I say.

"We'll look up a couple places when we get to Shelbie's house, okay? Once Violet gets to know you she won't care about it anymore. For now it makes you seem sophisticated and accomplished. Here, park in the driveway. Shelbie said it was fine."

I pull into the narrow space and park at an incline that seems perilous.

"Lovebirds!" Lehna calls into the backseat. "It's time to get out of the car!"

I hear Uma murmur something and June giggle, and then I guess some weird time-lapse thing happens, because the three of them are outside of the car and I am still here, clutching the steering wheel.

Lehna knocks on the window.

"Come on, *Kate*."

I follow them inside to where Shelbie and her cool city-dwelling friends sprawl across the sofas and rugs, laughing and drinking and looking fabulous. All these kids, gay and straight and everything in between—they look at us and wave and say hello and I would like to stop and get to know some of them, but Lehna heads to the study, where the computer screen saver glows, shifting family snapshots, and says, "We have to look something up real quick. We'll be right back."

And then, even though I am right behind her, she says, "Let's go, *Kate*."

I'm about to ask why it's so annoying to her; it's my name, after all. And it's not like I've decided that I want to be called something totally random. It's just another form of Katherine, one I think might suit me better. But I don't even need to ask her because I already know the answer. When you're friends with someone for such a long time, it's easy to feel like she belongs to you, like the version of the person you became friends with is the only real version. If she hated peas when she was a kid then she will always hate peas, and if she starts to eat them and declares them delicious, really she is deluding herself, masking her hatred of them, trying to pretend that she's someone she's not.

But the thing is, I never chose to be called Katie. As far as I know, that's what my parents called me the moment I popped out and I never even thought of the other possibilities until recently, when I started to feel like something was a little bit off every time someone said my name. And as I stand here in this dim room while Lehna looks up the names and descriptions of San Francisco art galleries I can't help thinking about how that applies to a lot of my friends, too. I didn't choose to be friends with Lehna. Not *really*. I kind of just fell into it the way you fall into things when you're a kid in a new school and the first person who pays attention to you feels like such a gift, such an overwhelming relief. You are not alone. You have a friend. And it's only later—maybe even years later—that you stop and wonder, *Why this person? Why her?*

Lehna rattles off the names of galleries, but I can see from the images on the screen that my paintings wouldn't belong in any of them.

"This is such a bad idea," I say. "If she brings it up I'll just tell her that you misunderstood me or something. I'll tell her that I *want* to have a show one day."

"It isn't enough," Lehna says. She turns in her swivel chair and looks at me. "You want this, right?"

"Yes," I say. "I want this."

And I can see how much Lehna wants it to work out between Violet and me, too. There must be some compromise we can reach, some in between. I lean over the computer and type: *hair salon art gallery san francisco.*

"Let's start out a little more realistically, okay?"

I find a trendy salon in Hayes Valley that features a new artist's work every month.

"Your stuff is way better than that," Lehna says, even though the work that they are featuring this month is actually really nice. Delicate line drawings with splashes of color. Mostly portraits, some botanicals. She clicks through some other links until she finds a list of San Francisco's best new galleries.

"Look through this," she says. "Choose one."

"Fine," I say, even though I know it's a terrible idea. Because what Lehna is telling me is that I'm not enough for Violet yet. I need to be better, and I know that I can be, even if I have to fake it for a little while. "But I don't have a show lined up yet," I tell Lehna. "It's still preliminary."

"Let's just say they went crazy when they saw your portfolio. It's only a matter of time." She reaches into her pocket for her phone and when she looks back up at me she's smiling.

"Violet's on her way," she says. "Maybe you could, like, reapply?"

"Yeah, okay."

I stand up and I find myself hot and dizzy, saying, "I think my lipstick's in the car," even though it's not.

We head out of the study and into the crowd that has already multiplied in the few minutes we spent back there. None of the faces are ones that I recognize, and they are now too absorbed in one another to acknowledge us. Lehna at least *looks* like she belongs with her nose ring and her hair in its ponytail to show off the patch on one side that she keeps buzzed short. June and Uma are nowhere to be found. They've probably snuck off to a bedroom.

"I'll be right back," I tell Lehna, and she nods and walks into the kitchen.

I step around the kids on the rugs and out the door, past my car, and up to the corner, telling myself that I'll just walk around the block. I need a few minutes by myself because I suddenly feel stupid and small and like there's no way I could be worthy of this girl I'm about to meet.

But I reach the end of the block and I keep walking, up through Dolores Park, into the throngs of celebrating people. They're a happy riptide and I'm letting myself get carried out, deeper and deeper into the sea of them, further from the moment I've been awaiting for so long.

Out here feels worlds away from Shelbie's living room. A bunch of teenagers sitting around looking cool is nothing like the thrumming swarm on the street. Here everything is electric and happy. Even the toughest-looking women, leaning against storefronts with expressions of practiced unapproachability, soften when I smile at them. Even the most aloof-looking boys seem sweet.

I don't know how long I've been walking and I don't want to take my phone out to check. I should turn back, but I'm not ready to leave all of this yet. Just thinking of Violet makes my hands tremble, and I'm standing next to the open door of a club that's beckoning me inside with the techno remix of an old jazz song. I reapply my lipstick in the darkened window—for myself, not for Lehna—and then I step inside. It's so dark it takes a minute for my eyes to adjust, but soon I spot the bar. I'll just try to get a drink, give myself some time to calm down. Then I'll walk back to the house, ignore Lehna's disapproval, and meet Violet.

The boy serving drinks is paper-doll perfect, and the crowd of men waiting to order from him seems to be in direct proportion to his attractiveness. But at the other end of the bar a cute girl with short hair and tattoos all over her muscular arms seems to be coming back from a break, so I make my way over to her and flash her a smile. She locks eyes with me and nods a nod that means she'll take my order.

I lean over the bar toward her until our faces are close. She tips her head to the side so that she'll hear my voice over the music.

"Tanqueray and tonic." Lehna learned this from her older sister and taught me how to say it with confidence. It's the only drink I know how to order.

The bartender turns away from me and grabs the green bottle and a glass.

I wish I had Violet's number because I would text her and say: *I got a little sidetracked and ended up in a bar. Meet me here?* I would say: *I've been really looking forward to meeting you.*

I avoid looking at my lit-up phone as I dig in my purse for my wallet. The bartender plunks my drink in front of me on a bright pink napkin, and I hand her ten dollars in exchange. Then I make my way to a tall table with a single bar stool. It's been shoved against a wall and left unoccupied, because everyone here is either standing or dancing, pushing their way into the center of the party. I take my first sip as the paper-doll bartender makes an announcement and cheering follows. It's for a contest; I can't hear what kind, but soon "Umbrella" is playing and almost-naked men are climbing on top of the bar. Some of them look superconfident, some of them look self-conscious, but they are all having fun and their happiness fills me up. I watch them strutting around and then I watch the crowd watching them, and I notice that most of the guys are focused on one particular dancer. I follow their gaze to a boy who seems too young to be in here but who also seems totally at home.

All he's wearing are those tight boxer things I've seen in Calvin Klein ads, red and blue, and with his close-cropped blond hair and general wholesomeness he could be the gay poster boy for America. Unlike one of the older guys who is practically humping the bar, he doesn't even seem like he's trying to be sexy. He's just doing his thing, singing along. I sing along with him. He points into the crowd and a dark-haired boy whoops back at him. And it's crazy, but I *know* that boy. He's a junior; his name is Ryan. He used one of my landscapes for the cover of the literary journal last semester. I couldn't tell if he was gay, but I guess this answers my question.

And now I'm starting to think that the dancing boy looks somewhat familiar, like I've seen him in a commercial or something, like he's played in the background while I've been thinking of other things. But no. I know him from real life, I guess, because he's caught sight of me now and his whole demeanor changes.

He freezes. *Mark Rissi!* We've never even talked, but we sit next to each other in Calc. Now the song is over and the crowd is going crazy. Mark jumps down from the bar and Ryan is trying to high-five him, but Mark is still looking at me, taking his clothes from Ryan and muttering something.

When Mark reaches my table, he's still fumbling with his belt buckle.

He stops in front of me and says, "Oh my God."

All of that confidence and happiness is gone, and I want it back for him. That *rush*. I want it back for all of us. I feel like we share something, in what we're missing right now.

"Hey, Mark," I say. "It *is* Mark, right?"

He nods, but all he says, again, is, "Oh my God."

"I have something serious to ask you." My heart is pounding because I'm not the kind of person who just opens up to anyone. I tend to be more of a listener, not a sharer of problems, but tonight is not a typical night. Violet is less than a mile away from us, the bass is pounding, the disco ball casting diamonds of light through the darkness, and it turns out that the shy jock from Calc is in reality a heartthrob jailbait of a boy who dances practically naked in gay bars.

"Please—" Mark starts.

But I am not a ruiner of squeaky-clean reputations. I'm ready to move on to bigger things with him. So I cut him off and say, "I thought it was an excellent performance. By the time you leave I'm sure that every available guy in here will have given you his number."

Ryan appears next to us.

"It's my fault," he says. "I kind of coerced him into doing it."

"God, you two," I say. "Lighten up! I won't tell anyone. But, Mark, just listen, okay? Because I'm about to ask you something and, like I said, it's a serious question."

Mark's panic fades into relief. He sighs and runs his hand over his face. When he looks at me again, he is ready to listen.

"Do you want to be friends with me?" I ask him.

He cocks his head.

"Come again?"

"I know that makes me sound like I'm in preschool or something. It's not even the main question, but I feel like we should establish a friendship before I ask you what I really want to ask you. I've spent the whole day, the whole school year, really, realizing that I might not actually like my friends all that much. Which is why I'm at a bar by myself on a night when everyone else is with other people. I wasn't supposed to be here, but here I am, and then here *you* are, and it's like a flashing arrow is pointing at you, telling me that you are someone I should know."

"Uhm," Mark says.

Ryan mutters something about invisibility, but I don't ask him what he means because I'm too focused on Mark's face.

"I guess?" he says. "I mean, if you want to."

"Okay, good. So now for the real question: Have you ever wanted something so badly that it sort of takes over your life? Like, you still do all the things you're supposed to do, but you're just going through the motions because you are entirely consumed by this one thing?"

The blush that was beginning to fade comes rushing back to his face, even deeper than before, and his eyes dart toward Ryan and then quickly away. *Interesting.*

Mark nods, and he really looks into my face as he does it, and I look hard back at him, and it is clear: We understand each other.

"I just ran away from a girl I don't know yet," I tell him.

He smiles. "She sounds that bad?"

"No," I say. "She sounds amazing. She's supposed to change my life."

"So what happened?"

"She's all I can think about all the time," I say.

"Yes," he says. He understands.

"Have you ever wanted something so badly that when it's about to happen, you feel this need to sabotage yourself?"

His eyes stay fixed on mine and I can tell that he's trying to follow me to this place, but he ends up shaking his head.

"No," he says. "I don't think I work that way."

"I didn't think I did, either. I've been waiting for this night for months. And then, I just . . ." I shrug. I feel my eyes well up.

"Wait, wait, wait," he says. "Don't give up. It's still tonight. Where were you supposed to meet her?"

"At this party."

"Okay, and is it close?"

"Yeah, just through the park and over a few blocks."

"Has anyone tried to get in touch with you?"

I groan. "I'm afraid to look."

"Then hand it over." He waits. I dig my phone out of my bag and place it, screen down, into the broad palm of his hand.

"Whoa," he says, the light of the screen illuminating his face. "Twenty-three texts from Lehna Morgan."

"Go ahead."

"Want me to read them all or just the highlights?"

"Just the highlights."

He scrolls down the list.

"They're mostly variations on 'Where the fuck are you?' A few 'Are you okay?'s.'"

"Keep going."

"One says: 'Violet just got here.' Is that the girl?"

I nod.

"Okay, hold on. . . . Oh."

"What?"

"She left. About five minutes ago."

"Is she coming back?"

"Lehna doesn't say."

I look into my drink. Mostly empty. Just some remnants of ice cubes.

"Maybe I should order another one."

"*Or* we could try to find her."

Mark's face is open, hopeful—a perfect antidote to the despair slowly settling in me. I'm about to ask him how we'd go about finding her, but the music gets softer and a man's voice booms out that the winner of the midnight underwear dance contest has been determined.

People cheer and I cheer with them, rooting for my new friend, Mark, who is not looking toward the bartender but is instead scanning the room, the hope on his face now mingling with concern as the bartender says, "Defeating our reigning champ, Patrick, *Mark* takes the crown tonight. Mark, are you still out there? Get your all-American sexy butt up here to collect your prize."

And then the music is loud again and everyone is dancing.

"Aren't you gonna go up there?" I ask him. "The prize

could be something good. You know, penis-shaped lollipops, rainbow-patterned condoms . . ."

But Mark doesn't laugh. He doesn't move. So I turn toward where he's looking and I finally spot Ryan, who is now across the room from us. He's with a few cute college boys, one with thick black glasses, another in a ski cap, and another who I can only see from the back, tattoos peeking out of his shirtsleeves, one hand holding a glass of beer, the other hand settled in the curve of Ryan's back. One song fades into the next and Tattoo Boy and his friends are feeling it. He turns, takes a few gulps of beer, sets the glass on a nearby table, and starts moving with the rhythm.

I've probably kept Mark to myself for too long. Here he is, out in the city on the kickoff of the year's gayest week, winning underwear contests, the object of quite a few lustful gazes, and I've trapped him in a corner with my crisis.

"You should go over there," I say, but Mark doesn't even seem to hear me. That despair I mentioned I was feeling? It's like it has suddenly become contagious, taken over Mark's entire body. His shoulders are slumped; his breathing seems labored.

"What is it?" I ask him. "What's wrong?"

"It's Ryan," he says, so quietly I can barely hear him. "He's dancing."

3

Someone is pulling me back to the bar. The bartender is giving me an envelope with fifty-seven singles in it and a gift certificate to a dry-cleaning service. Ryan isn't even watching. Katie's watching. Plenty of other guys are watching. But Ryan's on the dance floor, leaning into this guy whose arms are covered in words I can't read.

He's not doing it to hurt me. I have to believe that. He's doing it to make himself happy. Which just happens to hurt me.

I take my envelope and push my way back to Katie. Guys are putting their hands on my shoulder, telling me congratulations, using that as an excuse to put their hands on my shoulder, to see if I will stop and smile and maybe take things from there. I'm not stupid. I know this. I know I'm supposed to want this.

This room is so full of possibilities, I can imagine Ryan telling me.

Technically true. But the thing about possibilities: There are some you want much more than others. Or only one you want much more than everything else.

"What did you get?" Katie asks when I'm back beside her. I show her. She looks disappointed.

"Maybe you're supposed to get the bills dry-cleaned?" she says. "Lord only knows where they've been."

I notice the dry cleaner is called Pride Dry Cleaning. A few jokes pop into my head—*I can imagine what stains they're good at getting out* or *They specialize in rainbows*—but all the jokes are in Ryan's voice, not mine.

The dance floor is getting more crowded. I can't see him.

"I hope you don't mind me asking," Katie says, "but are you two . . . together? Because if you are, that's definitely a foul."

"No, we're not," I tell her. And then I think, *Fuck it.* "Only, sometimes we are."

"Your poor heart," she says.

"Yeah," I say. "Something like that."

I see him now. He's dancing with all three of them. I think of molecules, and how they're attached. I could probably join in. It's not like they've paired off.

"Should I go over there?" I ask.

"I have no idea." Katie studies the situation for a moment. "I think if I were him, I'd have to try really hard to avoid looking over here. He's like one of those waiters who's all attention during the meal, and then when you need the check, he'll glance every single direction except yours. You know what I mean? And if that's the case, then I'd say you probably shouldn't go over there."

A Florence song comes on. I love Florence. Ryan knows this. If he doesn't look for me during a Florence song, I am screwed.

I look over.

He's started to sing along. But not to me.

"Oh man," I say. The tattooed guy isn't singing back. But he's listening. He's enjoying it. They're both enjoying it.

And as they're enjoying it, this shirtless guy comes up to me, smiling like I know him.

I steal a glimpse of his chest, his abs. He looks like someone who may have dabbled in porn.

"Do I know you?" I yell over the song.

"No, but don't you want to?" he asks.

"Really?" Katie says.

But Johnny No Shirt isn't listening to her. He's focusing on me. Really. Intently.

"What are you doing?" he asks, more conversational now.

Where is your shirt? I want to ask. I mean, did he come here shirtless? Like, on the street? Or is there a shirt locker somewhere?

He has to be in his twenties. At least. And that's just not me.

"I'm heading out," I tell him. "Sorry."

This only makes him lean in closer. Playfully. Like, to the point that his jeans are touching mine.

"We have a girl to find," I say. "Violet. Maybe you've, um, seen her?"

He takes my hand and starts to guide it to his back pocket.

"She's right here," he says, smiling.

"No no no no *no*," Katie interrupts. "Thou shalt *not* take her name in that vein." He steps back and lets go, finally hearing her. She looks me in the eye. "As I see it, Mark, you're at a crossroads here, and there are at least three options you can follow. Well, four, because there's always the option of doing none of the options. I am not advocating one over the other. I just need to know what to do."

Johnny No Shirt has somehow gotten his hand on my back, and it's putting my body into a little bit of a trance. But I'm still looking at the dance floor, still watching how Ryan isn't watching. And then there's Katie, who looks much less amused than anyone else except maybe me.

"I'm coming with you," I say. I turn to my chesty suitor and tell him sorry again. This time, he relents.

"Some other time," he says. "I'll keep an eye out for you."

As he's walking away, I take a long look at his perfectly sculpted back. My whole body sighs.

"Are you sure you want to leave?" Katie asks.

"Yeah," I tell her. "I'm sure."

"But why? I mean, you own this place right now."

I look her in the eye. "Because we're friends. Duh."

That's enough for her. And it's enough for me, too.

We start to go, but I still feel the foolish pull of obligation, this strange sense that I'm abandoning Ryan. We were in this night together, and even if he's dancing with someone else, I can't leave without saying goodbye. But I can't go over there, either.

I send him a text. Tell him I'm helping Katie out with something and that he should text me when he wants to head back. I'll come meet him.

I hit *send*. I imagine the phone pressing against his thigh, signaling. But it can't compete with the music, can't compete with the dance or the boy that Ryan is now smiling at, leaning into.

"I have to go," I tell Katie. "Like, right now. I have to go."

The street is almost as crowded as the club. Pride Week is just starting, but nobody's holding back anything for Monday or Tuesday or any day after.

"So where were you supposed to meet her?" I ask. "I mean, that's where we should start."

Katie stops walking. "I know . . . but what if she's there?"

"Isn't that the point?"

"It is. But . . ."

"But what?"

"I don't want to just *run into* her. I need to be prepared."

"Do you know what she looks like?"

From the scalding look she gives me, it's clear she's *memorized* what Violet looks like.

"Okay. So we'll play this carefully. Keep our eyes open. If you see her, we take a time-out. Gather your thoughts. Go from there."

"But what if she isn't there at all?"

"Then we'll follow the trail, my dear Watson."

"Okay." She takes a deep breath. "Let's do it."

But she doesn't move.

"You need to lead the way," I remind her.

"Oh yeah," she says.

She still doesn't move.

I don't say anything. I wait. She closes her eyes for a second, says something to herself. Then we're off. We're back in the throng again.

I'm expecting to be dragged to a club with a feline name, where short-haired women lean laconically into each other with Brooklyn poses as they talk about love and compare their vining tattoos. All the lesbians I know are in some way smarter than me, or at least seem to know the world a little more. They also tend to read a lot of books.

But this party isn't at a club, it's in a house that looks like Stockbroker Sally could live in it. The people gathered outside are as drunk as anyone else—I wonder why I don't imagine lesbians as ever being drunk, as if they're just too smart or cool for that. There's a guy leaning out a window, yelling, "I love you! I love you all!" He is not looking at me or Katie when he says this.

"Friend of yours?" I ask.

"No," Katie says. "But they are." She points to two girls sitting on the curb. One of them is smoking, the other breathing it in.

We walk over. As soon as they see her, they jump up and let out a shared barrage of sentences.

"Where have you—"

   "*been?*"

"Lehna's been looking—"

   "all over for—"

"you. She, like—"

   "*so mad.*"

"Why did you—"

   "Where did you—"

"*go?*"

  They stop for a second and finally notice me standing there.

"Mark," Katie says, "this is June and Uma. June and Uma, this is Mark. He goes to our school."

"This doesn't look good," June says.

"No, this doesn't look good at all," Uma agrees.

Katie turns bright red. "Noooooooooooooooooo. I didn't leave to see Mark. I just met Mark along the way."

"Well, you missed her," Uma says.

"You really, really missed her," June adds.

"But where did she go?" I ask.

"What's it to you?" June asks me.

"What's it to him?" Uma asks Katie.

I feel my phone vibrate once in my pocket. A text.

"Excuse me for a moment," I say.

I'm hoping it's from Ryan. I'm expecting it's from Ryan.

But instead it's my mom.

Where are you?

This is not good.

I could lie. I want to lie. But she wouldn't be asking if she didn't already know the answer. A lie will only make it worse.

I'm in the city.

It only takes her five seconds to reply. She's better at her phone than I am.

Why are you in the city? Is Ryan with you?

This time I borrow a new truth to take the place of the original truth.

My friend Katie needed me. I'll explain tomorrow.

Then I lie outright.

And yes, Ryan's with me.

This does not appease my mother. She types:

If you are not on the next train home, your father is coming to get you.

I quickly text Ryan.

The moms have discovered our subterfuge. In other words, we're fucked. Need to get back ASAP. Meet me?

I expect him to respond immediately. But he doesn't. He must still be dancing.

I turn back to Katie and am about to tell her I need to go. But before I can get a word out, an angry Viking of a girl comes storming up to us and sucks all the air out of a ten-block radius, just to fill her lungs enough to belt out an enormous *"ARE YOU OKAY?"* in Katie's general direction.

Katie moves to answer, but before she can, the Viking continues. "Were you abducted? Lured away by a stranger with candy? Or maybe you saw a cat in a tree and felt you had to save it? Was there an old queen trying to cross the street, and you had to help? No, wait—I know. You heard about a top-secret Sleater-Kinney concert in an abandoned BART station, but you weren't allowed to tell anyone about it—not even your very best friend. That has to be it. Because if you are not bodily harmed, and if you were not at some secret show, or if you were not *saving someone's life,* why would you leave here *without saying a word* and then not respond when I call you and text you *a thousand times*?"

"Lehna," Katie attempts, "I just—"

Lehna holds up her hand, cuts off the excuse. "She was here, Katie. She was so excited to meet you. She brought you a flower, for Christ's sake. And there we were, going from room to room, looking for you. We even checked the closets because isn't that funny, ha ha ha, *maybe she's in the closet.* She watched as I called and texted you. I said you had to be here somewhere. I said you wouldn't just leave, because you were so excited to meet her. She believed me at first. But after a while, even I started to become unconvinced. Because you know what? You might as well have just slammed a door in her face. If you wanted to blow your chances this badly, why not just slam a door in her face?"

In the smallest, saddest voice I can imagine, Katie says, "She brought me a flower?"

I expect one of her other friends to pat her back, to tell her it's going to be fine. When none of them does that, I find myself doing it instead.

She's taking these deep breaths, like sobbing but without the tears. Like suddenly it's all too much.

"She can't have gotten far," I say. Then I look at Lehna. "Where did she go?"

"Who *the fuck* are you?"

"I'm Mark. Why *the fuck* are you so angry?"

"I am angry because after months of planning, after concocting a brilliant cover story and spending more energy on this relationship than I have ever spent on any of my own relationships, my best friend decided to bail. Even though she swore she wouldn't. Even though she made it look like she was going to go through with it for once in her life. My awesome cousin was willing to put up with Shelbie's hideous house music and even more hideous beer in order to meet this girl I had told her so, so many good things about. I am angry because this didn't have to happen, but then it happened anyway. I feel like a complete fool for thinking it could have been otherwise. And I feel like an even worse fool for getting Violet so excited and then having to tell her, Sorry, it isn't going to work, after all. I'd ask if this makes sense to you, fratboy, but I couldn't give *a shit* whether or not it makes sense to you."

"Stop," Katie says. "Just stop. It was my mistake. Not his."

"So you at least admit it was a mistake?"

"Why does that matter, Lehna? Really, why?"

Katie doesn't sound angry. Just tired. My hand remains on her back. She is leaning into it a little.

My phone vibrates again, still in my other hand.

"Sorry," I say, looking at the screen.

My mother.

Tell me you are on your way to the station.

Katie gives me a curious glance.

"My alibi's been shredded and my mom wants me on the next train home," I explain.

"I'll drive you," she says.

"You'll *drive him*?" Lehna huffs.

Got a ride back, I text. Then I check my messages. Still nothing from Ryan.

Katie steps away from my hand. Steps toward June and Uma.

"I'm sorry I left without telling you," she says. "I wasn't ready. I wanted it so much, and I wasn't ready for that."

June looks like she's going to say something, but Uma squeezes her hand and gestures her head in Lehna's direction.

"You're never going to be ready," Lehna says, her voice warming somewhat. "Don't you see that? You have to forget about ready. If you don't, you're always going to run away."

I almost feel like it's Ryan here, lecturing me. Except that my problem has never been about running away. My problem has been about staying in the same place.

"Where did she go?" Katie asks Lehna. "Just tell me."

Lehna shakes her head. "Not tonight. Not now. It's too late."

My phone starts to make itself known again. Once I see it's not Ryan, I leave it alone.

"I came back to see her," Katie says. "Don't you see that? I wouldn't be here if I wasn't ready to see her. I'm still scared, but I'm not *too* scared."

Lehna offers a hand, and I think for a second that this is it, Katie's won her over. But instead she says, "Let it go for tonight. Come in and have a drink. Shelbie's been asking about you, and I think she's still sober enough to register that you've returned. Plus, they have Tanqueray."

Katie leaves Lehna's hand hanging in the air.

"You're not going to tell me where she is? You know, and you're not going to tell me?"

Lehna pulls her hand back, wipes it against her skirt. "She moved on. She was disappointed, but she moved on. You should do the same. And we can see where we are tomorrow."

I'm figuring if I didn't see Katie at the club early on, odds are she wasn't there for much time. So this Violet didn't wait all that long before moving on, whatever that means.

Maybe Katie's doing this math, too. Or maybe she's feeling like I am—tired from this whole night, tired from all the drama.

"I think it's time for me to go home," she says. "I know I'm your ride, and I don't want to leave you stranded. But I really want to go now."

June and Uma both look to Lehna, to see where this is going next.

Lehna doesn't disappoint.

"Come on, Katie—"

"*Kate.*"

"Okay, *Katherine*—don't be like that. Don't punish us for

what you did. The night is still young and my mother is, I'm sure, too knocked out on sleeping pills to hear people come and go. We can get home at four in the morning and no one will notice. Don't ruin our night just because you ruined yours."

Katie pulls her keys out of her pocket and dangles them in the air.

"Are you coming?" she asks June and Uma.

June looks at Uma. Uma looks at Lehna, then shakes her head.

"We'll find someone else to drive us," Lehna says. "Or take a cab. I don't care. We're not leaving now. Candace is here, and I haven't even begun flirting with her. And Shelbie's brother is an awesome singer."

Katie tosses the keys up in the air, then catches them.

"Fine," she says. But the tremor in her voice shows she's not fine. She tried to call Lehna's bluff, but now she's the one falling off the cliff.

"I really appreciate it," I tell her. "You driving me home."

"Yeah," she says, looking me in the eye—trying to find something she needs in there, but I'm not sure what. "Let's get you home." She turns back to her friends. "I'll talk to you to-morrow. Or see you Monday. Whatever."

My phone reminds me it has messages. As Katie and I walk away, I check them.

From my mother:

Who's driving you?

And from Ryan:

I think I'm going to fly solo tonight. Well, not exactly solo. ☺ *Have fun, my friend.*

I stop in my tracks. I want to give up on the whole uni-verse. I show Katie the screen.

"Dickish," she says. "So dickish."

And the pathetic thing is: I want to defend him. I want to say that it's not sarcastic this time. He *does* want me to have fun.

Because he's having fun. Somewhere. With someone. And he wants me to have that fun, too. He does.

We've walked a couple blocks, out of range of the sounds of the party. So I'm a little surprised to hear footsteps running on the sidewalk behind us. Katie and I turn to see who's coming.

"June?" Katie says.

June is a little out of breath and speaks too fast at first. "I'mprettysureshewenttothewharf."

"What?" Katie asks.

June breathes in. Puts her hand on Katie's arm.

"The sea lions," she says. "She said she'd never seen the sea lions. So I think they're taking her to see them."

Kate

4

A tulip, a dahlia, a freesia, a rose.

I can't even think about what just happened, so I am thinking about flowers instead. About what a girl like Violet would choose for a girl like me.

"Of course we're going," Mark is saying. "It's not even that far out of our way. It's to the bridge and then a little past it."

"Thirty-nine piers past it," I say.

"Still," he says. "You need to do it. There's someone you think you might love who thinks she might love you in return. What kind of friend would I be if I didn't make you go after that?"

I am still not ready. Especially not now, after I screwed it up, slammed a door, made it so that our meeting will begin with an apology instead of a hello.

Lehna was right, though, when she told me I have to go right through it. Even I can see that. There are so many people in the world who are unlucky in love. I might be one of them, but that hasn't been determined yet. What if Violet turns out to be exactly who I want her to be? Or what if she is different, unexpected, in a way that's even better?

What if she really could change my life?

It would be a crime against love to not take this chance, so I send a silent thank-you to June and sail past the on-ramp to the bridge. Mark actually lets out a whoop as we pass it, like I just made some great play at one of his baseball games.

A daisy, a zinnia, a lilac, an aster.

As I list them to myself, I see a new series of paintings. Individual flowers against cobalt-blue backgrounds. If I paint them right, they'll look like more than pretty flowers. They'll look like the possibility of love.

The Embarcadero is dark and still. Parking, for once, is easy to find.

I turn off the engine and we get out. I can hear the sea lions barking, but nothing else. The quiet throws me off because I was expecting to find the pier crowded with tourists carrying souvenirs, their bellies full of clam chowder and sourdough bread.

But it's late and everything is closed. Mark must feel my worry, because he says, "She wasn't here to shop. She was here for the sea lions. Let's walk toward the water."

With each step, I feel a little hope escaping.

"What does she look like?" Mark asks, as if there's anyone here to distinguish her from.

I play along.

"She has short dark hair. In the pictures I've seen, it's usually falling into her eyes. In a perfect way."

He smiles.

"And she has really great cheekbones, and a tiny scar by her eye from a circus accident."

"A *what*?"

I laugh. I feel like he should already know everything; I forgot that he barely knows me.

So I tell him everything about her, which feels like telling him about myself, because when you think about something so intensely for so long, it kind of has a way of taking over everything else. I tell him about the circus and Mathilde, about the words Violet uses in the letters she writes. I tell him about a photograph I've stared at for hours, of her standing in front of a collapsing circus tent, with gold paint on her face and bangles on her wrist, her hand through her messy hair, the curve of her collarbone so gorgeous it hurts. I keep telling him about all of it even as we come to the end of the pier and the last traces of hope disappear.

I keep talking so that I won't cry.

And then I've said all that I know about her.

We sit on a bench overlooking the sea lions sleeping in heaps, the bay to one side of us, the city with its empty, towering buildings to the other. All of the photos of her, all of the stories, all of the facts spin in a loop in my head, but I spare him a second round of the monologue. I look toward the bay, but all I'm seeing is that photograph of Violet. The tent is billowing in the wind, the fiercest red. She's looking straight at me, wondering what I'll do next.

Mark and I must have been destined for each other, because what two-hour-old friendship can endure such a deep silence? Eventually, his phone vibrates.

"Your mom again?" I ask.

He grimaces.

"We can go."

"I'll try to make the last train. You might still be able to find her."

"No," I say. "We should spare me from subsequent chances to let myself down."

He nods, and then he leans forward and puts his head in his hands.

"I'm sure you aren't in *that* much trouble," I say.

"It isn't that."

"Oh," I say. "Right."

"I keep seeing him with those guys. I keep wondering what he's doing. Who he's doing it with. And, as far as he knows, I should be home by now. I can't believe he hasn't even texted to see what kind of heinous punishment my mother is inflicting on me."

"Well, if it's any consolation, Tattoo Boy has nothing on you. Pretty much every guy in that bar shared my opinion."

"Unfortunately, there's only one opinion I really care about at the moment." He peers up at me. "Sorry," he says.

"No, I get it," I say. "And what will happen next? He'll call you tomorrow and tell you all about it and you'll have to act happy for him? Or will it be more like he calls you and talks about the weather and, like, his plans for the literary journal next year?"

"I don't even know. This is uncharted territory for us." He looks across the water, to the bridge looming above us. "But what if he does want to swap stories? What if he tells me all about his awesome night with the college guys and all the college hipster parties he went to after the bar, where they drank beers out of mason jars and spun records or something? Then he'll ask me what I did and I'll say that I ruined your night and made you drive me home and then got lectured by my mother before going to sleep."

"That's bleak," I say.

I run through a similar scenario in my head. Lehna and June and Uma telling me all about how wild the party got, where they went afterwards.

There has been an undercurrent of trouble between Lehna and me for a while—the way I've been wondering about our friendship, the way small things that I do annoy her. But what just happened was entirely above the surface, and we're not used to that. The number of real fights we've gotten into before this night is a perfect zero. I always took for granted that someday we'd be these bickering old ladies drinking iced tea on a porch somewhere, bragging about our grandkids. I'd think mine were cuter than hers and she'd still sound snarky every time she said my name.

What just happened between us was serious, and the fact that I left makes it so much worse. They count on me to be there. I'm never the difficult one who vetoes the restaurant choice or doesn't want to go to the movie because I've seen it already. There is always something to like on a menu, some new meaning to glean in a film. Maybe the fact that I'm easy is the reason I'm their friend. Now that I've let them down, they'll probably get a ride home with someone who will become Lehna's new best friend. She'll be this fearless girl whom Lehna will never have to lecture, who will never disappoint her.

"Okay," I say. "It's bleak *and* it's unacceptable. We're going home, but we're also going to have the time of our lives."

"How?"

"We're going to make up an excellent story to tell in the morning."

He laughs.

"What kind of story?"

"Well, we know what Shelbie's party is like. And we have a pretty clear idea of what Ryan is up to. So we just have to top those. We can vouch for each other."

He shoots me a skeptical glance, but I can see he's considering it.

"All right," he says. "Fuck it. At this point I'd do just about anything to avoid further humiliation."

"We need to come up with a scenario that is basically their dream, and then fill in the details," I say. "Like Lehna loves her San Francisco connections. She's into the status of it, the fact that Shelbie lives in a Victorian near Dolores Park. That she goes to a private school and spends the summer in France. Like somehow Lehna is more sophisticated by association. So we should make it about something superclassy. Like a party in a mansion in Pacific Heights."

"Wow." Mark laughs. "We're really going for this. Okay, let me think."

We stand up and make our way past the dark touristy restaurants and the souvenir kiosks, their metal roller doors pulled down for the night.

"Ryan really likes art," Mark says. And even though he should be pissed off, he sounds so earnest, like he's just telling me about this boy he loves instead of planning a lie that will make him jealous. "I mean, *The Arts.* So if this party were to include, like, artists and writers and people like that, he'd probably feel like he missed out."

"Perfect. So we went to a Pride party in a mansion

owned by a couple of superrich, artistic guys. And they had a foyer full of sculptures that were so obscure they were almost impossible to look at. But then the sculptor himself was a guest at the party and he explained them all to us and now we understand everything there is to understand about art."

In all the minutes we've been here, there hasn't been a trace of any other person. I'm beginning to wonder if Violet even made it here. Maybe she got sidetracked by a better plan, or went to see the sea lions at a different pier even though this is the one famous for them.

And then Mark says, "Oh, fuck."

"What?"

He's stopped walking, is looking at something on a bench where the pier ends and the sidewalk begins.

It looks like a flower.

Slowly, we approach it, side by side.

A rose.

Of course.

Bright red. Like the circus tent in the photograph, like the lipstick I was told to reapply for her. I reach carefully and pick it up between two fingers. She removed all the thorns. I could hold it tight in my fist if I wanted to.

"What does it mean?" I whisper. "That she would leave it here? Was she throwing it away?"

"She might have been," Mark whispers back. "But maybe not. Maybe it was an act of hope, like when you make a wish, send it out into the world."

"You hope it finds its way back to you," I say.

"Yeah."

"If she wanted to throw it away, she would have put it in

the trash or dropped it on the ground, not set it here where it wouldn't get stepped on."

I say it with a certainty that I wish I could feel, but as I speak the words, they make sense. So I hold the rose's thornless stem tightly. We climb into the Jeep and I set it on my lap because I am a cautious driver who keeps both hands on the wheel, but I want to keep this flower close to me. To part with it feels like bad luck.

And now we are on the on-ramp and officially leaving the city. Unlike our drive here, nothing about being on the bridge fills me with awe. There is nothing beautiful about it. We're on the lower deck, surrounded by no one because it is only midnight and no respectable party would be even remotely close to over. I keep thinking, *How could we have missed her?*

"But how did we end up at this party?" Mark asks, bringing me back to our plan. "Maybe some painting connection of yours? Like, have you ever had any cool art teachers or something?"

I shake my head. It's true—how would Mark and I ever end up at a party like that? This was a bad idea. No one will believe us, and the more we plan, the more distance we cover, the farther we get from the city, from Ryan, from Violet, from all my friends who might not even be my friends anymore, from the electric current of the night and the possibility that my life might change.

"Actually," Mark says. "I totally know how we could have ended up at a party like that."

And then he pulls a business card out of his wallet and tells me about this world-famous photographer who just happened to ask him if he modeled and also *took his picture* and gave him his card.

"How *on earth* was this not the first thing you told me tonight?"

"Everything was such a blur," he says. "And, you know, I've been kind of preoccupied. But I should text this guy and find out if he really is at a party, because it would suck if we used him as an excuse and it turned out Ryan saw him somewhere else."

"Yeah," I say. "Good call."

Mark sends him the world's longest text, reintroducing himself, providing some distinguishing characteristics to remind the guy in case he's taken pictures of quite a few could-be models tonight, saying that the night has stalled out, and asking if there's anything cool going on.

"If he writes back I'll just say that we'll try to make it. And then I can tell him that it didn't work out."

"Good plan," I say, but as I say it I glide over two lanes and slow to take the narrow, curving exit onto Treasure Island.

"Where are we going?" Mark asks me, and the truth is that I don't know. But it isn't home. Not yet. As I pull onto the side of the road, the awe is officially back. The city glows so close in front of us. I can almost hear the voices of hundreds of thousands of celebrating people.

"Hand me the phone," I say.

He doesn't ask me why; he just does it.

I find his recent calls and tap *Home*.

"What's your mom's name?"

"Becca," he says. "But, to be honest, I don't think—"

"Becca!" I say to the voice that answers. "This is Kate Cleary. I'm a senior in Mark's Calc class, and I also happen to be his chaperone this evening. I'm calling to touch base with you about our plans."

"Are you the person who is supposed to be driving him home right now?" Becca asks me. Her voice is so familiar even though I've never heard it. It's the stern but kind voice of a TV mom. I don't yet know her, but I *know* her. And so I carry on.

"Yes," I say. "And, in fact, we are in the car now, and we will absolutely keep driving home if that's what you need. But I have to say that the night is young, Becca, and we are, too."

"Is this on speaker?"

"Just a second. Now it is."

"Hey, Mom."

"Mark?"

"Yeah, Mom."

"You remember your SAT workshop starts tomorrow, right?"

"Yeah, I remember."

"I want you to get the most out of it."

"Yeah, I will."

"Kate, how did you do on your SATs?"

"All right."

"Where are you going for college?"

"UCLA."

"Oh," she says. "Wow. And *what* class are you in with Mark?"

"Calculus. I got into their art program. There was a portfolio review, so the SAT scores matter less. But they were fine; they were decent."

"Maybe you could help Mark this summer."

"Mom."

"Vocabulary drills, maybe?"

"I'd love to," I say.

"*Mom*," Mark says.

Becca sighs.

"So what do you think?" I ask. "We don't even have any plans. We're just enjoying the energy. It's extra celebratory this year. Any chance we could get an extension on the evening? Just a *few* hours?"

"Normally I would say no to this. It's already so late and you *snuck out,* Mark."

"You snuck out?" I shake my head at him in mock disappointment.

"Sorry," he says into the phone. "You know. Desperate times? Or something?"

"Wait," she says. "Where's Ryan?"

"He, um . . ." Mark is searching for an answer and I don't want him to get himself into even more trouble by covering for his sometimes-secret-boyfriend, other times heartbreaker-of-a-best-friend. But it's his call, not mine.

"He's asleep in the back," he finally says. "It's just Katie and me awake now."

"Okay. You can have a little more time. But *only* if you stay together."

"I'm the ride," I remind her. "So he's stuck with me."

"Two hours from now at the latest. And that is firm."

Mark's jaw drops.

"Awesome. Thanks so much, Becca!"

"Okay, Kate. Come around the house soon so we can meet in person. Mark, have fun and be safe. I love you."

We hang up, and Mark says, "Two hours from now? Are you my fairy godmother? Is this Jeep actually a pumpkin? I didn't even know my mother was capable of establishing this kind of curfew. I wasn't sure this hour was a time she knew existed. Like, maybe theoretically she knew, but I certainly didn't think she would know from experience, like from actually looking at a clock and seeing that it was *this late* and she was still awake."

"Don't underestimate your mother."

We both look out at the city. All of those lights, all of that darkness. I touch one of the rose's petals. Violet is out there, somewhere.

"So," Mark says. "I'm pretty sure you're babysitting me."

"Yeah. I wasn't going to say anything about it, but that's definitely the impression I got."

"That's kind of fucked up. Thanks, Mom. Thanks so much."

"Well. Desperate measures, I guess."

"So what now?" he asks, and right then his phone lights up.

"The photographer?"

He nods.

"He's at a friend's party in Russian Hill." He turns to me and swallows, a grin spreading across his face. "He gave me the address."

MONDAY

MARK

5

It takes a day for it to hit. I guess people are tired or something.

But when it hits, it *hits*.

By Monday morning, it feels like everyone in school has seen. Or at least the people who care about such things. Which includes Ryan.

The blog—the gossip one that everyone reads—calls me an It Boy. The life of the party.

This is open to interpretation. Some of the interpretations include:

I never realized how hot he is.

I heard he's on drugs.

He must be dating that photographer.

He must be sleeping with that photographer. After all, they're both gay.

You'd never guess that such a quiet guy parties so hard.

It's too bad he isn't straight—I'd date THAT in a second.

Even I can acknowledge that the photo's amazing. I can say this objectively because I can't really believe it's me.

Everybody wants to know the details about what happened or what didn't happen to It Boy and Rising Art Star.

I don't know if Ryan finds the link on his own or if someone forwards it to him early Monday morning, knowing we're friends. I do know, however, exactly when Ryan first sees it, because a few seconds later I get a text from him:

WTF? I think there are some things you have to tell me.

As if he's told me anything about his weekend. As if I heard from him at all on Sunday.

I'll see you at school, I text back.

But at school it's not Ryan I'm looking for—it's Katie. It's so strange to think that she's been here the whole time, walking the same linoleum halls, without me ever really knowing her. I wonder if she's a member of the GSA, or if there are invisible pockets of lesbians who meet in empty classrooms throughout the school, under the radar of gay boys who are too caught up in their own drama to notice. I myself have never been to a GSA meeting, partly because it wasn't something I could do with Ryan and partly because I usually had practice at the same time.

I guess Katie and I have formed our own rainbow alliance. It feels like she's something I've always wanted but didn't know I wanted until I got it: a partner in crime.

In all the craziness of Saturday night, I didn't think to get her number and put it in my phone. I don't even know where her locker is. But when Sara Smith comes up to me and says, "You two. Wow, you two," I know she isn't talking about me and Ryan. I ask her if she's seen Katie, and she points vaguely over her left shoulder, which is enough to guide me.

Katie looks to be at the same level of surprise I am—something short of shocked but far past surreal.

"This is insane," I tell her. "I mean, the plan was to get to Ryan and Violet. But now everyone else is a part of it. Sort of."

"Have you heard from him?"

"Sort of. Have you heard from her?"

"No. Just Lehna. Who's livid. She actually called me *ungrateful*."

"Did she ask you what really happened?"

Katie shakes her head. We swore that we would only tell them what really happened if they thought to ask.

We're betting on the fact that they won't. And living on the hope that they will.

"May I make a confession?" I ask, even though I would never say such a thing if I didn't already know the answer was *yes*.

"Please," Katie says.

"I would just like to state for the record that I wish you could stay at my side all day, so we could go through this together. Whatever this ends up being."

Katie looks at me with what I think is amusement.

"What?" I ask.

"It's just that you're such a softie. I never would have called that."

"Why?"

"Because you're on the baseball team? Because we've never said three words to each other until this past weekend? Because, in general, I've gotten a bro vibe from you whenever I've seen you in the halls."

"You've seen me in the halls?"

"You see, *that* was more the kind of comment I would have expected you to make. A small masterpiece of handcrafted obliviousness, delivered with sincerity."

She's saying this, but she's not saying it critically. I think.

She looks at my expression and chuckles. Then she pats me on the arm.

"Don't worry. I'd love for you to ride shotgun with me, too. But I'd also like to graduate, and that makes class attendance mandatory. I'll see you in Calc, though. Think you can fend off the paparazzi 'til then?"

"I guess I'll have to get used to having my picture taken."

She gives me another brief pat on the arm, then heads off to first period. I feel a little more alone without her, which is strange.

I catch some people looking at me during Spanish, but mostly it feels like things are returning to normal. But then second period is study hall, and that's where I know I'm going to see Ryan. It's one of the parts of the day that I've always designated as our time—all we have to do is tell Mr. Peterson that we're going to the library and he'll let us leave; the fewer kids he has to watch over, the happier he is. Sometimes Ryan and I ask for permission at the same time, but mostly we space it out. He doesn't want it to seem like we're running off together. And as long as the end result is us running off together, I never mind.

It isn't completely out of the question for us to head to the library. We'd sit across from each other, and the tension there made everything—even a pencil sliding from my side of the table to his—seem powerful and ours. Other times, we'd break free from the building and walk through the woods or the playing fields. If it was absolutely quiet—if there was absolutely no one around—I could usually get him to make out with me a little. And when it was done, he'd smile and start talking again as if nothing had happened, as if other people were around, even when they weren't. Everyone knew we were friends, so we acted like friends. But that's never what it felt like, not if I was being honest with myself. I wanted him more than that. I needed him more than that.

By the time I get to the room, he's already got the pass in his hand. He winks at me and steps into the hall. I go to Mr. Peterson and ask for a pass of my own. He actually questions me about why I need to go to the library. *Of all days, why do you have to start being skeptical now?* I think. But I also answer quickly, invent a report on Sylvia Plath that I'm researching. He grunts at the mention of Sylvia Plath, as if she's an ex-girlfriend of his. But he lets me go.

Ryan is waiting just outside the doorway, just out of Mr. Peterson's line of sight. He looks eager to see me. And, despite everything that happened Saturday night, this eagerness makes all my hopes feel a little more justified.

"Well well well," he says, smiling and shaking his head. "It looks like both of us had nights to remember."

If he were just my friend, I would smile back at this. I would be curious. I would want to know everything.

But I don't want to know what he means. And I can't think of any way to tell him that.

From the direction he starts walking, I know we're headed to the cafeteria, not the library.

"Taylor told me—he said that when he saw you dancing on the bar like that, he knew you'd have no problem finding some trouble. I was a little worried, when I saw you weren't in the club anymore, but he told me you'd be fine. And then, you know, he was kissing me, and I didn't worry as much."

"Taylor was the one with the tattoos?" I find myself asking.

Ryan nods. "Yeah. Some you could see. And some weren't apparent until . . . later."

I don't want to know what this means. I have to know, but I don't.

"But holy shit, me getting to know Taylor is nothing compared to you partying it up at the Facetime Mansion. Do you know how many of my favorite authors hang out there? Please tell me Zadie Smith spilled her drink all over you."

I try to give him my best Mona Lisa Smile. His question, in my mind, doesn't count as asking. He's not asking to hear about me. He's asking to hear something that would reflect back on him.

We're at the cafeteria now, but instead of going outside like we usually do, he steers us to a table. No one is around, except the staff starting to put lunch together.

"I have to tell you, Taylor was awesome," he says as he sits down—but not before double-checking that even the lunch ladies can't hear us. "I promised him I'll be there for the real Pride Week festivities, now that kickoff is over. So we have to go back. It is absolutely imperative that we go back."

"I'm sure that can be arranged," I say.

"I owe you my life for covering for me. I don't know what you told your mom, but it worked—she didn't rat me out. I didn't get home until about three o'clock on Sunday, and I was sure my mom was going to be waiting in the front room with this huge magnet, and she'd make me watch as she fried my phone and my laptop. Or she'd make me read only James Patterson until I left for college. Something really cruel like that. But she wasn't even home! She'd left me a note—*Hope you and Mark had a good night. I'll say we did!*"

He is happy for me. I remind myself that he is happy for me.

The first time something happened between us, I wasn't expecting it. We were in his basement, playing some game that was half racing and half mortal combat. I was handing his ass to him, and he wasn't taking it too well. The bloodshed on the screen started to spread into the room. I'd slam his vehicle into a ditch and he'd poke me in the ribs. I'd crash into his vehicle's side and he would use his body to crash back into me. Finally, the fifth or sixth time this happened, I threw down my controller and attacked full on. Laughing and shoving, ducking and pushing and yelling out hyperbolic threats. Before I knew it, we were rolling on the floor, and he was on top of me, and we were still laughing, but there was also something serious in the way he was looking at me, and something serious in the way I was feeling that look. He had me pinned, and then he eased up a little, settled down a little. And now it was something else. I had wanted it for a long time but had never imagined I would get it. I kissed him first—I know I kissed him first—but it didn't feel like I was kissing him first, because I was only confirming what I had already seen, what I suddenly knew. We kissed, and it was awkward afterwards, awkward when we were sitting up again, awkward when our minds had to give what we were doing a name. I thought it was the end of the world, but it wasn't. I thought it was the start of the world, but it wasn't. Instead it was an introduction to the halfway world where we'd spend the next two years.

And now . . . he's so excited, he's practically beaming

that we didn't get caught, and I don't want him to be happy for me.

I want him to be happy *with* me.

But I don't know how to get there. I've never known how to get there.

"I swear," he goes on, "I had no idea how much fun that was going to be. Leave this place behind and try something else on for size. Or some*one* else, ha ha. You know how I am. More than anyone, you know how I am. So I'm sure you can appreciate it when I tell you that you have one hundred percent won me over."

"To what?" I ask.

"To adventure! To the city! To *pride*, ha ha."

I know I should be asking him more about his night. But the best I can do is, "So you told Taylor you were in college?"

"Nope. I told him the truth. How weird is that? And even weirder? He skipped kindergarten, so he's only a year older than me. Not that he was looking for someone from high school. Honestly, I think he made his approach partly because he saw me with you and was sure you had to be in college to be on the bar like that. You wild man, you."

He's being playful, even appreciative. But it feels just as crummy as snarkiness would.

"You know what?" I tell him. "I almost forgot. I actually have to go to the library. For this report. About Sylvia Plath."

"Oh, I'm sure they'll have a Plathora of material for you," he says. I get up, but he doesn't do the same.

"You coming?" I ask. I still want to be with him. I just don't want to be talking about his weekend right now.

"Nah," he says, taking out his phone. "I'm going to stay

here and chat a little with Taylor. He was texting me during first period, but Ms. Gold's ruthless when it comes to phones in her class."

I should leave him to it. It shouldn't really matter. But it matters. Some pride in me won't allow me to pretend it doesn't.

"So are you two, like, together now?" I ask.

He raises an eyebrow. "Because we're texting? Are you with Katie Cleary now because you went to a party together? It is what it is, and I don't know what it is yet. I'm just trying to get to the point where I see if I can find out. 'Til then, it's just flirting."

"And what about us? Do we just stop?"

He looks at me, genuinely mystified, and says, "Stop what?"

"Nothing," I say. "Never mind."

I walk away before I can say anything else. I wanted him to be the jealous one. But now I'm the jealous one. The jealous and confused one.

I head to the library because I can't think of anywhere else to go. I wish I knew where Katie was. I wish there was a way I could text Ryan and have him be as excited by that text as he'd be by one from Taylor.

Dave Hughes, a guy from the team, sees me walk into the library and waves me over. I wonder if he's going to ask me about the party and the mansion, but it ends up he's just being friendly. He asks me how my weekend was. I tell him it was fine. He clears off some of his stuff so I can sit down. I put my head down and try to sleep.

"Good ol' Monday morning," Dave says.

I nod on the desk.

"It's gonna get better," he tells me. Because that's what people say.

I am already mapping out the rest of the day. Usually lunch would be the next significant part, because that would be the next time I'd see Ryan. But now I'm not sure. I'm thinking I should skip it. I wish Katie had the same lunch period as me. But I'm going to have to wait until sixth period to see her.

I hope she'll have better news than I do.

Kate

6

When we were little kids, Lehna and I painted a mural in my garage. It's a fairy-tale scene, a little too Disney for my taste now. There are towers and dragons and a multitude of girls with long hair. There's a prince, but I swear the prince is really a girl in disguise. I've never seen such a delicate boy. In the sky, hovering over a castle, is my name. On the other side, over one of the dragons, is Lehna's. It's that simple. No *and*, no *friends forever*. Just this:

KATIE LEHNA

Right now—as I stand in front of my locker knowing that Lehna will show up at hers any second and that when she does we'll have to either look at each other for the first time since I drove away or, even worse, *not* look at each other—I think of all the tiny details we painted. The rings on the fingers of the princesses. The scales on the bodies of the dragons. So many rays of the sun, and so many blades of grass, and so many tiny pairs of shoes that hover above the ground because we didn't want the colors to mix or smudge.

I spent most of yesterday in the garage, staring at it. I had to move all these boxes and plastic bins away from the wall so that I had a clear view. My parents had no idea what I was doing. They kept walking past the open garage door and pretending not to look in, maybe hoping I'd taken on an epic task of organization, only to discover that I was sitting on a bin of Christmas decorations, staring at a wall.

I took a break for lunch. Ate a sandwich in the driveway in the sun.

At around three, my mom came in carrying her laptop.

"Aunt Gina just called. Your photo is on *The Daily Dish*! It's not *of* you—don't get too excited—but you're in the background."

She kept holding the laptop out, trying to show me, but there were so many boxes between us that eventually she just held up the computer and pointed. The screen was at the wrong angle. I couldn't see anything, let alone myself.

I smiled.

"Cool," I said.

And then I turned back to our mural, unsure of what I was hoping to find there.

And now, here is Lehna, spinning her combination next to me.

"You wanted to see me?" she asks, because just as we both know she has History next period and that tome necessitates a trip to her locker, we also know that I have Volleyball and need precisely nothing from mine.

I nod, but she isn't looking.

"So what do you want to say?"

My mind is blank.

"Did you see me in *The Daily Dish*?" I ask, without meaning to.

She slams shut her locker and narrows her eyes at me.

"I mean, it doesn't really matter. The picture wasn't even supposed to be of me. I didn't actually even see it; I just wondered . . ."

She looks past me, down the hall.

"I have to go. Class starts in, like, two seconds and I need to text Candace."

"Candace!" I say. "So what happened? I can't believe I forgot."

"I can," she says.

"Lehna," I say. "Really. Can't we just get over whatever this is? I want to hear about Candace."

"I really have to go. I can tell you at lunch. Unless, of course, you're going to be hanging out with your new best friend."

"Mark isn't in our lunch period," I say, which I guess is the wrong response, because Lehna shakes her head and stomps down the hall with such finality that I don't even consider going after her.

On my way to the gym I see Ryan leaving the teachers' lounge, carrying a stack of literary magazines.

"Last issue of the year," I say, catching a glimpse of the

cover. I recognize the work of Elsa, a quiet girl in my AP Studio Art class who makes intricate collages.

"Oh wow," Ryan says. "I'm no longer invisible."

I laugh and continue walking, but he stops me.

"Hey, um, actually . . ."

And I know where he's going to go with this, and I realize there was a scenario Mark and I didn't plan for.

We know that we aren't going to volunteer information about Saturday night unless Ryan and Lehna ask us directly. But we were assuming that Ryan would ask *Mark,* that Lehna would ask *me.* What do I do if the reverse happens? I am not good with quick decision making. I'm much better at obsessing for so long over a decision that the answer becomes irrelevant.

"Did Mark say anything about writing an essay on Sylvia Plath?"

"Oh," I say, confused. "An essay? It's a little late in the year, isn't it?"

"Exactly," he says. "At first I was like, *Yeah, Sylvia Plath puns!* But then last period I thought, *Wait a second. It's review week. No one's writing essays.*"

I shrug. "You probably just misunderstood."

"Probably," he says, but I can tell he's unconvinced.

"All right," I say. "Volleyball time."

"Okay, but one other thing."

Shit.

"What exactly happened Saturday night? I mean, not that it's a huge deal, but . . ."

He looks self-conscious, and I understand why. Mark is his best friend; he shouldn't need to ask me. The way he's trying to be casual while actually looking desperate is embarrassing to both of us.

I fight the urge to run away.

I decide against lying.

But I decide, also, against telling the whole truth.

"Magic," I say. "A cat named Renoir. A whiskey bottle. A typewriter. Ferns. High-heeled shoes."

He arches an eyebrow.

I smile.

"Volleyball," I say again.

I step past him, and I don't look back.

I take my time changing out of my gym clothes after Volleyball is over. Some girls loiter around me, wanting to ask me questions, but maybe the worry on my face is enough of a deterrent. They give me shy waves and goodbyes as they leave, and then it's just me in the empty locker room. Two minutes of silence.

I wish I knew why I felt so sick.

I wish my brain wasn't constantly counting down the days until high school is over.

Or, if that's inevitable, I wish every day that passed lessened the pressure in my chest instead of intensifying it.

I finally get myself back outside, onto the path that will take me to the senior deck where Lehna and Uma and June will be basking in the sun with their lunches. And soon there they are, at a distance. I slow down to look at them.

What will I say?

June and Uma are each nibbling sandwiches while Lehna talks, gesturing grandly about something. I wonder if Lehna and I would become friends if we met each other today. If we hadn't had hundreds of sleepovers, if we'd never painted murals in my garage, if we didn't stand next to each other, hands clasped and hearts swelling, at that Tegan and Sara concert in eighth grade.

If Lehna and I were to find ourselves, strangers, standing in a line in an art store or a café, would we each think enough of the other to start a conversation? And would we laugh at the things that were said?

I honestly don't know.

June and Uma, yes. Now they are changing positions, sitting so that their backs are together, June's short black curls against Uma's blond waves, each using the other for support. If I saw them, let's say, getting burritos after school, I would find them irresistible. But even that certainty doesn't feel like enough right now. An initial spark isn't enough to sustain a friendship. June and Uma are the kind of couple who can't even have a one-on-one phone conversation. They always put me on speaker. And their voices sound so alike that I rarely know who is saying what, which used to bother me before I realized that it hardly mattered. They're practically conjoined anyway.

Uma catches sight of me. She waves. And guilt crashes in. These are my *friends*. I walk down the steps to the wide, wooden deck and sit next to Lehna without looking at her.

June and Uma turn their faces to the side to look at me, cheek to cheek with their backs still pressed together.

"Hi, Rising Art Star," June says, smiling at me behind glamorous sunglasses.

"Hi," I say back, grimacing in a way I hope shows that I don't take myself that seriously.

Lehna pulls a peach out of her bag and takes a bite. She

holds it out to me. It's such a tiny gesture, but it makes me swell with gratitude, and that makes me want to cry.

I'm so confused.

I take a bite of her peach and hand it back.

"I want to hear all about Candace," I say.

"She's totally in love with Lehna," Uma says.

"I don't know about that," Lehna says. "We talked, though. We talked for a long time."

"Three hours," June says. "That's an epic conversation."

"What about?"

Lehna shrugs.

"Everything," she says. "College. The future. Everything."

I nod, but as she tells me more all I think about are the conversations that she and I have *not* been having. About college, about the future. The one where I tell her how afraid I am and how this new fear scares me. The one where I confess that I don't know how I got into UCLA's art program, because I'm sure my work isn't good enough, and once I get there they're going to find me out. I'll be laughed at; I'll be humiliated. And the one where I tell her that *nothing* about college excites me: not the dorms or the dining hall, not the possibility of a great roommate or great parties, not the classes that will supposedly blow my mind or the memories that will supposedly stay with me forever. *Nothing.* I feel like a fraud every time anyone asks me where I'm going. They are always impressed, and I always feign excitement, and all the while I'm trying to stop time from passing, stop summer vacation from coming, stop classes from ending, stop everything.

"She's going to Lewis and Clark," Lehna's saying, "which is great because Portland isn't that far from Eugene, so we could meet up on weekends. She can't decide whether she wants to major in history or math. She knows she wants to be a teacher. Can you imagine being just as good at history as you are at math? She's so smart."

"Cool," I say, trying to sound enthusiastic, but I wonder if she can see through me.

I feel like she should, because friendship is about more than facts. It's about knowing what someone is thinking, or knowing enough to know that you don't. But I guess it's also about not letting too much time go by without asking them questions, so you don't end up looking at them one afternoon, the sun so bright you have to squint, realizing that you hardly recognize the person they've become. Maybe, when it comes to friendship, both of us are getting this wrong.

"Holy fuck," Uma says.

"What?" Lehna and I ask in unison.

June doesn't have to ask, because Uma is showing her something on her phone. Both of their jaws drop.

"Katie," Uma says.

"Kate," June says.

"Have you been on Insta today?"

I shake my head. I've been avoiding my phone.

"You have, like, five billion new followers."

Uma shoves her phone at me, and it's true. Where I used to have a modest number of followers, mostly people I know in real life and some friends I've made online, now the number doesn't even make sense to me. There are way too many digits. I click on my latest picture—an elephant painting—and there are over three thousand likes.

"What the fuck?" I say. "Look at this."

I hold the phone out to Lehna. It takes her a moment too

long to take it, but she has no other choice. She looks. She frowns. She scrolls through the pictures and comments until she stops and her eyes narrow.

"AntlerThorn says: 'Rumor has it a show with the fabulous Kate Cleary is in our future. . . .'" She hands the phone back to Uma. "That gallery was on the list I found. The best new galleries? How did they . . . ? How did you . . . ?"

She stares at me, waiting.

I could tell her about Garrison Kline and his friends and how they promised to work magic for me, but Lehna isn't asking out of real interest or curiosity. Instead she seems angry, as if the art show wasn't her idea in the first place. I barely looked at her stupid list.

"Isn't this what you wanted?" I ask her.

She turns away.

The bell rings before I can say anything else, and we all stand up and gather our backpacks and lunch remnants and try to ignore the tension between us.

Today is a studio day in Art. All I have to do is paint. I block out the world with my headphones and Sharon Van Etten.

I begin something new.

Squeeze paint from tubes. Mix the color of a circus tent, a sky at dusk.

Violet.

Fifty minutes disappear with my brush on the canvas and the thought of her, and then I am washing the colors down the sink and Elsa stops next to me to return a tube of glue to a drawer.

"Finally," she says. "The tent."

"What do you mean?"

"All semester you've had these circus elements. The elephant with the star; the tightrope; those hoops on fire. And now, finally, the tent."

"I didn't know it was so obvious."

She shrugs.

"I wouldn't call it obvious. I'd call it a theme."

"Thank you," I say. "And, oh, the cover of the journal looks great."

"I was afraid they weren't going to get it printed on time. I mean, we get *yearbooks* tomorrow. We have four days and then it's over."

I dry my brushes. I try to keep breathing. But the thought of my last yearbook, full of goodbyes from everyone I've known almost all my life, leaves me shaken as I make my way to the math hall. Each minute is bringing me closer to a future I'm not ready for.

But then I see Mark. And I feel better.

I sit next to him at the desk where I've sat every day for several months, but for the first time I turn to face him.

"Hi," I say.

"Hi," he says.

We smile.

"I may have blown your cover," I confess. "I saw Ryan."

Mark's smile wavers.

"He asked me about a Sylvia Plath essay."

"Hm."

"Sylvia Plath wasn't in our plan. I am all for bending the truth for a worthy cause, but I can't say it comes naturally to me. But did I get you in trouble? I hope not."

He leans back in his chair.

"Who knows? At least he asked about it, I guess."

"Did he ask about anything else?"

"Not in a way that made me want to answer. Did she?"

"Not really."

"Well," he says, "it can be our secret for a little longer."

Ms. Kelly tells us we'll need to take notes, and soon we're all unzipping backpacks and digging for pencils.

"Please say you can hang out after school," I say.

"Definitely," Mark says.

Ms. Kelly begins her review, and Mark and I turn toward the board.

I stare at equations, copy what she's written, but soon I drift back to Violet.

MARK

7

When I find Katie after school, she looks completely freaked out.

"What?" I ask. "What is it?"

She holds up her phone.

"It's AntlerThorn. AntlerThorn wants me."

"Wow," I say. "Antler Thorn, huh?"

She nods. "AntlerThorn's already sent me a graphic to post to Instagram. So I posted it. This is so surreal."

"It most certainly is. I just have one question."

"What?"

"Who's Antler Thorn? Because I wouldn't have pegged you as the type to be getting calls from gay porn stars. And Antler Thorn sure as hell sounds like a gay porn star."

"It's a gallery. The one Garrison told us about, remember? AntlerThorn. One word."

She says this as if it makes much, much more sense as one word.

"That's awesome, right?" I say. I don't know much about the art world, but having a gallery want you must be like being scouted by the majors, at least.

"It *is* awesome. Except it's also weird. Because it's a lie that's coming true. The only person who thought I was having a gallery show was Violet. And now a gallery wants me to have a show there."

As we head to her car, she explains more of the backstory. I do not tell her that I am slightly distracted thinking of some of the outfits that Antler Thorn, Gay Porn Star™, would wear. I'm not sure she'd appreciate that.

I also know that Ryan would. I almost want to text him and ask him what he thinks when he hears the phrase *Antler Thorn*.

Then I imagine him responding:

Let me see what Taylor says.

I have to stop. I am spiraling into ridiculousness.

We're at Katie's car now. She points to this big, big zip-up envelope thing sitting on the passenger seat.

"I want you to look through those and pick the twelve I should show them."

We get in the car and I tell her, "I'm not sure that's the best idea. Ryan's the art person, not me. If you want to go through it, I'm happy to drive. . . ."

She shakes her head. "If I try to go through it, it will take me about twelve hours, and at the end of the twelve hours I'll be certain I am the most pathetic excuse for a non-artist in the history of everything. That's just the way it is. And we don't have twelve hours—I am supposed to be there by four.

Because they're doing this show of queer artists, and apparently one of the photographers had to take down his pieces because they were all reproductions of his cheating boyfriend's Grindr chats, pictures included, and the boyfriend is threatening to sue."

"Fortune does have a strange way of smiling, doesn't it?" I say, unzipping the carrier. She's going to have to drive fast if we're going to make it downtown by four.

I really don't know anything about painting. I don't know whether the colors I see are right or if the shapes make sense. I couldn't tell you which painters Katie is like or what style she's painting in. But almost immediately I can tell one very important thing about Katie's paintings: She means them.

I feel like I'm reading her journal. A journal made of poems, where the spaces and word arrangements are just as important as the words themselves. These paintings are not still lifes. There is nothing still about the life within them. Everything she's pictured has elements that are present and elements that are missing—you feel the presence and the absence and have to figure out whether the figures are almost complete or just starting to dissolve. A rope stretching across the sky, with a girl trying to balance atop it. The rope is solid, but neither end is attached to anything. In another painting there's a girl peering into a ring of fire. You can see her face all around the hoop, but when you look inside it there's a starry sky where her eye should be.

A Pegasus with only one wing, turning toward the ground.

A starfish with a missing limb ... but it's the missing limb that you feel reaching toward a comet.

A lion with a whip for a tail.

An elephant trying to curve its trunk around a crescent moon.

And then, in the next painting, the crescent moon trying to curve itself around the elephant.

She's painted these things as if every single one of them is real.

"I should turn the car around, shouldn't I?" Katie says when I've been silent for too long.

"Don't you fucking dare," I reply.

Katie seems satisfied by this.

"It's just a lot for me to take in," she says. "It's one thing when your friends are seeing it. Or people at school. But with strangers—it opens up something else. It gives a whole different dimension to it. Because suddenly the art has to stand for itself. That's weird to me."

"You've had plenty of scrimmages with your team, but now this is the game," I say.

"Yes. This is the game."

I sense there's something else she's not saying. So I go, "And?"

"And . . . I can't help thinking it's tied to her. None of this would have happened without her."

"None of it would have happened without you, either."

"I know. But I guess my point is that it's the combination. Her and me equals this. However directly or indirectly. This."

We drive a while longer, letting Sky Ferreira and Lorde do the singing for us. I finish looking at her art—even though I'm strictly amateur, there are some pieces that can be eliminated easily. Rough sketches that are rough because they haven't found their subject yet. Assignments that feel like assignments.

A collage that's supposed to be political but only ends up being obvious.

"Have you made your choices?" Katie asks.

I can't believe she trusts me. But I nod anyway.

"Good," she says. "Keep those in the portfolio and throw the rest in the backseat."

"Are you sure?" I ask.

She looks me in the eye and says, "Never."

AntlerThorn is located in a somewhat trendsidential area off of Japantown. If it has a name, I don't know it. All I know is that once we're inside the gallery I am way, *way* out of my element. EDM is blasting Every Damn Moment, and the walls are painted the brightest pink I've ever seen.

"Intense," I say.

"That's one word for it," Katie murmurs.

The music cuts off. The lights undim. A Mumford & Sons song begin to strum in the far background.

A man comes out of a door in the back and tells us, "Hello, hello, *hello*!" He's got a grizzly beard and a Tigger bounce as he walks. He's wearing a One Direction T-shirt, on which someone has spray-painted *AND THAT DIRECTION IS OUT.*

"You must be Ms. Cleary. And entourage. Audra is so sorry she can't be here to see you. I'm afraid you're stuck with me. LOL!"

"Hi," Katie says.

"Oh, how rude of me! I'm Brad. *Bad*-with-an-*r*! Or *rad*-with-a-*B*! Depends on which day you catch me! Can I get you something to drink? We have tap water, tap water, or tap water.

We're a nonprofit, after all. Not that we're a charity—we just rarely turn a profit! Ha!"

"I'm fine," I say.

"Me, too," Katie says.

Brad spies the portfolio in Katie's hand. "Oh, goody! Audra just *loved* what she saw on your Instagram—she wasn't going to take Garrison's word for it! We always like to check the work in person before committing to it. It's like online dating!"

Katie is starting to take deep breaths.

Brad talks on. "Sorry about the techno onslaught when you came in—Audra just wanted me to check it out for the opening tomorrow night. It's *so* great that you can take Antonio's place—I can't believe Ross is being such a *bitch* about it, but you know, Ross was always jealous of Antonio's art, in the same way that Antonio was jealous that Ross was sexting dick pics like they were spam. To each his own! Audra was so worried about the whole situation, and then you fell right onto our gaydar, and suddenly it was like, eureka, now we know what to do with Wall Six. 'Get 'em hung!' Audra told me. And I told her, 'I *try!*' Ha!"

He's walking us over to a table in front of a blank wall that must be Wall Six. I'm thinking I might need sunglasses to calm the power of the pink, but Katie isn't looking straight on. She's looking to the wall next to hers.

"Lin Chin," she says with something approaching awe in her voice.

Each piece on this wall is a glass box, and inside each box is a pair of folded paper cranes. At first I don't get it, but then I look closer, and my mind skips a beat. Because the cranes aren't just floating there. They aren't lifeless paper things. They exist in relation to one another. They are having a conversation, and I am observing it. Their bodies have language. The space between them has an intimacy.

"Oh yeah, aren't those great?" Brad says. "Lin made those especially for this exhibit, if you can believe that. She and Audra go way back. Wayyyyy back, if you catch my drift. Wayyyyyyyyyyyyyy back."

As Katie marvels at the cranes, Brad takes the pieces I've chosen out of the portfolio and spreads them on the table.

"Ooh!" he says. "Oh yes. Hmmm. Fierce. *Very* fierce."

Katie is pretending not to be listening, but it's obvious that she is. I turn to another wall to find a series of sketches of two men kissing. It starts when they are young—probably twelve or thirteen—and then, gradually, they age. Almost year by year. They're my age. Then they're older than me. And older. Their haircuts change. (One of them goes from blond to brunette to something in-between.) Their faces alter slightly, starting full, then narrowing, then regaining the fullness in a different way. The one thing that doesn't alter is the intensity of the kiss.

There isn't any explanation. Just the artist's name, Nic Pierce. But I don't think I need an explanation. I know, instinctively, that this has happened, that this is true. Nic Pierce found it. The kiss that lasts for years.

"Wow!" Brad says. I turn my head and see he's gesturing Katie over. I go over, too, because I feel she wants me by her side.

"These are *so fierce*," Brad tells her. "I mean, so, *so* fierce."

"Fierce," Katie repeats. "To be honest, I don't even know what that means."

"Ha! You are so *adorable*. The bottom line—and I'm a bottom, so I'd know, ha!—is that Audra loves your work.

Adores it. Have you sprung fully formed from the head of Cindy Sherman? No. Is your work on par with, say, Lin Chin's? Ha! But you have more promise in your little finger than most people have in their heads, and Audra just *loves* how many followers you have. Buzz always greases the wheels of art, and our wheels need all the lubrication they can get! You leave these with me and I will get them framed lickey-split—I know a guy who owes me some favors, and his framing's better than any of the other favors he could offer, ha! It's too late for us to get you in the catalog—sorry about that—but we can send out a release pronto that you've been added to the show, and the hits will follow. I promise: The hits will *definitely* follow."

"Can I have a minute to talk with my manager?" Katie asks.

"Sure!" Brad chirps. "Especially since he's cute as a butt. I mean, *button*. Ha!"

Katie yanks me over to the front of the gallery. We're now near a wall that has what I'd call the *c* word written in different fonts. It's very strange to see it in Comic Sans, but I guess that's the point.

"It is very unclear to me whether they are truly interested in my art, or are simply interested in my followers," Katie tells me. "And it's also very unclear to me whether that matters."

"I think he genuinely likes it," I tell her. "I mean, he finds it fierce."

"Catwoman is fierce. Cate Blanchett playing an assassin is fierce. Lady Macbeth is fierce. I'm not sure my art is supposed to be fierce."

"He did say *wow*. That's less ambiguous, right?"

"I just don't know if I'm ready for this. Am I ready for this?"

I want to tell her, *How am I supposed to know?* I want to point out to her that the only reason I've even looked at the lit mag was because I knew it would mean a lot to Ryan if I did. I want to pass the buck to someone who knows her better.

But I also want to tell her what she needs to hear. So I simply say, "Yes. You're ready for this."

She doesn't question my credentials. She doesn't thank me. She just nods and says, "Violet thought I was going to be in an art show. Now I'm going to be in one. I can't accept it, but I will anyway."

"That's the spirit," I tell her.

"Are we good?" Brad calls out.

"We're good!" Katie calls back.

Brad squees, then says, "Ooh, Audra will be so pleased. She has such an eye for talent. *Such* an eye. This will make her so happy. And when Audra's happy, we're *all* happy! No wire hangers! Ha. I think I'm going to break out some sparkling apple cider. Who's in?"

"We are!" I tell him.

He runs into the back room and returns with three plastic cups and a bottle.

"It's always good to have something on hand for special celebrations with the underage!" Brad proclaims. At first it looks like he's going to open the bottle over the table where Katie's art is lying, but she body-blocks him. Which is good, because when he pops the cork, the contents geyser onto the floor. "Ooh, that's always happening to me!" he giggles.

Eventually he gets some into the cups. As he does, I tell Katie, "I'm excited to be here. This is a big moment, right? Your first gallery showing."

"This is happening, isn't it?"

"Yup. It's happening."

Brad hands over the cups. "I'd like to make a toast!" he says. "Even though there are no true beginnings in life—there's always something that came before—there are definitely moments that feel like a beginning, and it's always good to stop and take a second to enjoy them. Your talent started long before you walked in that door, Katie, but here's to the start of a different, wider recognition of that talent. To Audra!"

"To Audra!" Katie echoes, while I say, "To Katie!" Then we clink our plastic cups and sip the warm cider of our celebration.

Katie looks like the kind of happy that doesn't believe itself. And I'm a more straightforward happy to see it.

We're so caught in the moment that we don't hear the door open. We don't sense anyone else in the gallery. It's only when she says, "Excuse me? Are you open?" that we turn to look.

I see a pretty girl with a sequined scarf looking somewhat confused.

Katie, however, sees something else.

"Violet?" she says, her fingers clutching the plastic cup so tight that it cracks.

"Kate? Is that really you?"

And Katie says, "Yes—I guess it's really me."

Kate

8

She's smiling her amazing smile, right here, right in front of me, not in a photograph, not on a screen, but *here*. In life.

And I am frozen, lukewarm cider dripping down my arm from my cracked cup, Brad saying, "Here, let me clean you up," and then, in Mark's direction, "I've never said *that* to a girl—ha!"

"What are you doing here?" Violet asks. But before I can answer she shakes her head and says, "I take that back. I only asked because I'm nervous. You're here because of your show. And *I'm* here because of your show. I saw your Instagram post, and I live not too far from here, and I wanted to see your paintings up close, without all the other people."

"How perfect," Brad says, dabbing my elbow with a paper napkin. "Are you a collector? So *sneaky*. So *smart* to just pop in the day before the opening. Bad girl! And by that I mean *good* girl. Feel free to take a look around. Kate's work is clearly fierce, but if it isn't quite what you're after I'd understand. I mean it's, you know, *wow,* but let's say it's not your cup of tea? If that's the case I'd be thrilled to introduce you to some of our other artists' work."

"I'm here to see Kate's work."

He stops dabbing and sets the napkin next to my tight-rope painting. Practically *on* my tightrope painting.

"Of course," he says. "And here it is."

His gesture toward the table may as well be the unveiling of my heart. The stripping off of my clothes.

I might as well be singing her a love song.

She walks toward them and I feel myself step backwards, away from the sight of her looking at my paintings. They are not fierce. They are not wow. They are crude representations of the possibility of love, and they were meant to remain secret. I didn't know it before, but I know it now. I mean *constellations*? How trite. I don't even know their names. I'm always confusing Cassiopeia with Perseus and they really look nothing alike.

My stomach drops. My hands tremble. I don't know how I got into the UCLA art program. I don't know how Violet—or anyone else—will find these paintings anything but amateurish.

"Open your eyes," Mark hisses. "You are acting *really* weird."

I didn't even realize they were closed, but now I'm seeing pink again, and when I brave a glance at Violet I think I may see her smiling, but I'm not sure because the door chimes and a woman swishes in.

"Audra, you're back!" Brad croons. "Look who showed up? It's Kate Cleary!"

Audra's hair is styled in a severe ponytail. Her eyeliner is catlike and everything she's wearing is covered in fringe. She faces me, stoic.

"Look, Kate, didn't I tell you she'd be thrilled? Here are the paintings, and they are even better in person!"

Violet steps aside to let Audra take her place before the table, where she studies them one by one and then gives a single nod before pulling her phone from her pocket.

"I knew you would just adore them!"

"The show's tomorrow night," Audra says. "What are you thinking about price?"

She's looking at her phone, but when no one else answers I assume this question is meant for me.

"Oh," I say. "I hadn't even thought about it."

"Please tell me they're for sale. I can't waste my time with artwork that isn't for commerce."

"No, that's fine," I say. "We can sell them. I just don't know how much I should charge."

Brad says, "Well, each of the Lin Chin crane boxes is three thousand, but—"

Audra snorts.

"Precisely," he continues. "And Nic's are eight hundred a drawing, though we agree they should all be sold to the same buyer. Breaking up that sequence would be worse than breaking up that couple! Anyone who disagrees is a *homewrecker*. Tabitha's Word-That-Rhymes-With-Shunt pieces are each a grand, a steal considering that they're high-concept *and* made of LED lights. Form meets function and all that. But Kate's not exactly in Tabitha's league."

Audra rolls her eyes.

Even though they asked me to be a part of this show, I feel like they don't want me in it. And that makes me want to back out, but how can I, now, when it would seem like it's all about the money? I know that I'm no Jenny Holzer; I'm no Banksy. Nothing I'm doing is revolutionary. But are my paintings really worth so much less than lit-up slang for genitalia?

"Four hundred is the most we can ask for a virtual unknown," Audra says. "And even that is a stretch."

Against my will, my eyes begin to burn. I'm blinking fast, trying to keep the tears away. This whole idea was so stupid, and I am angry at Lehna, angry at myself, angry that after all the moments I dreamed up it's *now*—when I am utterly humiliated—that Violet has entered my life.

"As her manager—" Mark begins, trying to save me.

"I'd like to buy them."

Audra and Brad freeze. Their heads tilt in synchronized intrigue.

"All of them," Violet says. "And I'm sorry, but I don't buy paintings priced below five hundred apiece, so I insist on paying that amount. The extra hundred goes directly to the artist."

"Well, technically the breakdown is fifty-fifty of the *total* amount," Brad says.

But Audra holds up a hand and, with that, Brad is silenced.

"That's very generous," Audra says. "And I assume you're comfortable with still having them hang in the show?"

"Oh, sure," Violet says. "As a favor to *you*. Kate doesn't exactly need the extra exposure."

Audra's mouth tenses, but only for a moment.

And now, instead of fighting back tears, I'm staring at

Violet in amazement. Here she is, with her short, messy hair and the tiny scar by her eye. With the scarf Lehna told me about and the mouth I dream about at night. But also with a clear voice I hadn't yet heard, and posture a little more slouchy than I'd imagined, and a slightly rounder face than in my tent photograph.

She is who I imagined and she is not who I imagined.

"One thing, though," she says, her head cocked, looking at the blank pink wall where the paintings will be. "Do you have those red dots? The kind that mean the painting's been sold?"

"We typically just mark the price sheet."

Violet grimaces. "Oh, that's disappointing."

"We can get red dots," Audra says.

We spill out of the gallery and onto the sidewalk, Mark and Violet and me. We make it around the corner before collapsing in laughter against the side of a building.

"My mom is going to kill me when she sees her credit card bill," Violet groans. "At least she's on a different continent, so my death is not imminent. Hey," she says to Mark. "We didn't formally meet. I'm Violet, Lehna's cousin."

"I'm Mark."

"My manager," I add.

"Right," she says. "Manager."

"Yeah," Mark nods. "And Katie's my SAT tutor."

"Interesting arrangement."

"It is indeed," Mark says.

"I feel like celebrating my first major art investments. Who wants sushi?"

Mark and I raise our hands.

The restaurant feels peaceful even though almost all the tables are occupied. There's no music playing, only the murmur of voices, and the light is perfect, not too bright. The hostess appears with three menus and leads us to a corner table, Violet right behind her, Mark and I following.

"Should I disappear?" Mark whispers. "This place seems kind of romantic."

I shake my head. "I want you here," I say. "I need you."

"Whoa," he says. "I'm flattered, but you know I don't think about you that way, right?"

I jab him in the ribs with my elbow and he yelps. Violet turns to us and raises an eyebrow.

I smile. Mark shrugs.

We take our seats. I am grateful that the table is round so we don't have to decide who sits next to whom.

I want to sit next to her, but I'm afraid to. I want to feel her close, but I want to see her face.

Our waitress arrives with tea and fills our little cups. As soon as she turns away, Mark pulls out his phone and positions it above the table.

"Oh no," Violet says. "You're one of *those* people? You can't just drink your tea—you have to Instagram or tweet or Facebook it?"

"No," he says. "I just have to text it."

"Text it to who?" I ask.

"You know who."

"Seriously?"

"Who's you know who?"

"Ryan," I say. "His best friend slash sort-of boyfriend."

"Oh!" Violet says, eyeing him. "I did *not* call that one. But okay. Sort-of boyfriend. Tell me about that."

"Not even sort-of boyfriend," Mark says. "*Former* sort-of boyfriend."

"Ouch. Go on."

He looks at me, and I'm not sure why, until I realize that the beginning to this story involves last Saturday night when I was supposed to be meeting Violet but instead found myself watching Mark dance almost naked in a bar.

"I want to apologize," I say. "Last Saturday got . . . complicated for me."

She smiles, but I can see some hurt behind it.

"Yeah," she says. "From Shelbie's house to the Facetime Mansion. I guess I assumed you'd have a story to tell me someday."

"Yes," I say. "Someday. But for now, I'll just say that I found myself, by chance, in a bar during an underwear-only dance contest, of which our friend Mark here was crowned the winner."

And from there the story unfolds and expands, stretching into the far past, how they met, how it felt, and the more recent past, how they kissed, how it felt—and the future Mark saw for them until Saturday night, when the sight of Ryan dancing in the bar shattered it.

"This is heartbreaking," Violet says. "Really. I feel for you. But please, *please* do not send this boy a picture of tea."

"You think it's pathetic?" Mark asks. "I know, I know: I should be ignoring him. He'll probably get this text and just wish it was a text from Taylor. He'll barely look at it." He lifts the cup and smells it. Sets it back down without sipping. "But the thing is that Ryan really likes tea. Especially green tea. And I never drink this stuff. So maybe it'll get his attention or something."

"Right," I say. "Like he'll wonder who you're with. Or in what ways you're changing. You'll become mysterious."

"Kate. Mark. Seriously. *Tea* is not going to make you mysterious. This is what I want you to do. Think of one sentence—just one. It has to be the truth. It has to come from your heart. Now go ahead and write it, but don't press *send* yet."

As he's thinking, the waitress returns and we place our orders. When she leaves, Mark enters something into his phone.

"Okay," Violet says. "There is something you should know about me. I tell stories with morals. I am going to begin one now."

Mark and I nod our approval.

"So there was this guy I knew in the troupe. Lars. He was maybe in his thirties and he was a lion tamer. A real natural with the animals; he was never even afraid. In addition to being fearless, he was a romantic. One night he told me about this girl he once knew and loved when he was a little kid. Like a *long* time ago, when he was eleven or twelve. Her name was Greta, and in the beginning of spring she told their class that her family was moving away, that that was her last day there. She cried as she told everyone, and he felt overcome by his love for her. He went home and he wrote her a poem and he delivered it to her on her doorstep. He can recite the whole thing, but I only remember one line, which translates into *Your silky flaxen hair glints golden*. It sounds terrible, I know. He assured me it just loses its effect in the translation, but I'm not so sure. *Anyway.* In every town we stopped in for a circus show, somewhere close to the fairgrounds where we'd set up camp, that line would appear spray-painted on a wall somewhere. I finally asked him about it. I said, 'What if Greta sees it one day and she remembers it, remembers *you,* and she wants to find you, but she can't?' Most of the performers didn't use their real names, and Lars was one of them. If she tried to look him up she would have found him untraceable. And I thought, if he still thinks about this girl from his childhood *so* much that he's scattered notes for her on buildings all across Europe—if he wants to reach her that badly—why wouldn't he leave her some kind of clue so she could find him?"

"And what did he say?" Mark asks.

"He said that I was missing the point. Finding each other was not the point. What really mattered, according to Lars, was that she knew."

I lean forward. "Knew what?"

"How much he loved her. How he still thought of her. He had this fantasy that she'd be going about her life somewhere in Berlin or Madrid or Oslo. She'd be walking her kids home from school, or buying bread, or heading home from the office and she would see that line scrawled across a brick wall, or a wood fence, or a billboard over a train track. A love letter. She would think of him. She'd remember her younger self. It might change her life. Or it might not."

We're quiet. Our soup arrives. Steam rises and we take our first cautious sips.

"The moral," she says, "in case you haven't come to it yourself, is that sometimes it's enough just to put something out into the world."

"So I'm supposed to send this text."

She nods.

"You *must* send that text."

He takes another sip, sets the bowl back down, and stares into it, brow furrowed.

"But Taylor," he says. "There's no way Ryan will ever choose me over Taylor."

"You can imagine what might happen after you press *send*," Violet says. "But you don't get to control it. And it could surprise you."

He looks at me, waiting.

"As your SAT tutor and your friend, I feel that I have an investment in your future," I say. "And I think you have to gamble in order to win."

MARK

9

It feels great for about three seconds.

Katie and Violet are excited that I've done it, I can tell. And that makes me happy, to have pleased them.

Then the bottom falls out.

What.

Have.

I.

Done?

If Apple really wants us to become addicted to their products, if they really want them to be the zenith of user-friendliness, why in Jobs's name isn't there an *unsend* button? How hard would it be to enable us to take it all back, to erase the mistake before it's seen?

What.

Was.

I.

Thinking?

What kind of spell did Violet cast that made me write what I just sent?

I will fight for you.

From what strange place did that rise up? How could I think, for even a moment, that this was something Ryan would want to receive?

What a Foolish Frederick I am.

Violet's still proud of me—she's completely unattuned to my rising panic. But Katie can tell something's wrong.

"What is it?" she asks. "What did you say?"

I pass her my phone. She takes one look at the message and says, "Goodness." Then she passes the phone to Violet, who reads the message and returns it to me.

"Is it true?" Violet asks.

"Is what true?"

"Would you really fight for him?"

I nod. But the nod isn't enough, so I add, "I would fight for him." And that's still not enough, so I go on. "In fact, I would tear through rubble with my bare hands to get to him. I would lift cars. I would wrestle down anyone who said we shouldn't be together. Because if you want to know the truth—if you *really* want to know the truth—none of that could be nearly as hard as being in love with him and not able to tell anyone about it. Including him. I have this *thing* inside me, and it's angry and it's scared and it's uncertain and most of all it's so completely in love with him, and it would do anything to keep him, even if it means things staying the way they are now."

I cannot believe I am telling them this. Why am I telling them this?

Before I can stop myself, I push further.

"I can't let him fall in love with someone else. I can't let it happen. Not like that. I am so mad at him and I am so in love with him, and it hurts to be realizing it like this. Would I fight for him? I have been fighting for him for years. And I'm losing. No matter what I do, I'm losing. But I have to fight anyway."

I want to laugh, because right now, sitting across from me with such matching concern, Katie and Violet look like a perfect couple. Exactly what I don't have. Which makes me do the opposite of laugh.

"You've never told him," Violet says. It's not a question. It's obvious.

"I tell him all the time—I just make sure it's never when he's listening. I say it when he's in the other room, or when he's asleep, or when the music's really loud. Sometimes he asks me what I just said. And I tell him never mind. Or I make up something else, something that isn't 'I love you.' "

I know talking about a problem is supposed to make you feel better about it, but talking about this only manages to make it feel more present. All my words, all this talk, is balanced out by the silence of my phone.

No reply.

No reply.

No reply.

Unsend.

"You can't keep it inside," Violet offers.

"Or maybe I can't keep it at all," I tell her. "Maybe it was never really mine in the first place."

You can be naked with someone and remain unknowable. You can be someone's secret without ever really knowing what the full secret is. You can know he's even more scared than you are, but that doesn't make you any less scared yourself.

We would draw lines, and then we would cross them. Underwear was going to stay on. We were going to mess around but not have sex. We were only going to have sex once, to see what it was like. We were not going to make it a big deal. We were not going to let it affect our friendship. We were not going to tell a soul.

I don't think he's said a thing to anyone.

I imagine he told Taylor that I was his friend. His wingman. His best friend.

If Taylor even asked.

Katie says my name gently, draws me back. She's looking at me carefully, while Violet watches my phone with a mix of surprise and horror at its inactivity. Maybe when she puts texts out into the universe, they come back to her quickly. Maybe she really thought her plan was going to work.

The waiter has probably been hovering for an hour, waiting for the teary gay boy with the phone problems to compose himself long enough to order more raw fish.

"Do you need anything else?" he asks.

I feel enough time has passed for my tea to get cold. But it hasn't.

I shake my head. I'm out of words until some more appear on my phone.

"Ryan could be busy," Katie says once the waiter's gone. "His phone could be off."

But my words will still be waiting for him.

And if he's half as into Taylor as he seemed to be, his phone is going to be within reaching distance and the ringer will be set loud enough to wake the dead.

Unless he's with Taylor right now.

Katie is reaching for my hand, but it's Violet's hand she should be reaching for. Here they are, together for the first time, and I've turned them into minor characters in my own soap opera.

"I always wonder what it would be like to meet him now, as a stranger," I find myself saying. "This is my game within our game—to try to come up with the scenario in which it would work out better. Maybe if I met him now. Maybe if I met him in college. After college. Once he's comfortable with who he is. But every time I do this, I feel awful. Because I'm sacrificing our history. I don't love him for who he is now. I wouldn't love him for who he is two years from now. I love him for all the hims he's already been with me. I guess that's the contradiction. I want a fresh start. I would fight for that fresh start. But I also want it to be a continuation."

Violet smiles. Not a happy smile—a melancholy smile.

"It's actually not a contradiction at all," she says. "You want the continuation that feels like a start."

At that moment, my phone vibrates on the table.

I'm afraid to look.

It's Katie who picks it up. Who reads the screen. Who says, "Oh."

"Is that a good 'oh' or a bad 'oh'?" I ask.

She holds up the phone so I can see it.

I'm glad you have my back.

I check the time he sent his message against the time I sent mine.

There's a six minute, forty second difference.

It took him six minutes and forty seconds to type: *I'm glad you have my back.*

I start to compose my next line. *I'm glad you're glad.* No. *Any time.* No. *Don't you know what I mean when I say I'll fight for you?*

No.

"Put down the phone," Violet insists.

"I wasn't going to—"

"I'm serious—put down the phone. Now. I know about these things. He's not done. He just needs to realize he's not done. And if you respond, you will prevent him from realizing that."

"How do you 'know about these things'?" Katie asks.

"Songs of innocence, songs of experience," Violet replies.

I can tell Katie is not entirely satisfied with this answer. She's about to say something, but she's interrupted by the phone vibrating again.

I need you, it says.

More typing. And then:

Come over?

I look at Katie and Violet. They look at me.

We all know what I'm going to do.

Kate

10

Now there are two of us at a table set for three.

And I guess the reality that Violet is here is finally settling in, after the humiliation of Brad and Audra and my paintings. After the giddy high of Violet's purchase, and the bravery of Mark's text, and the dreadful anticipation of Ryan's response.

Now it's just Violet and me, and I'm searching for something to say.

"So tell me about the trapeze. Is it scary?"

"It must be terrifying. I've only been on one a couple times, though, and only when it was very close to the ground."

"Your scar, though. I thought . . ."

"This?" She touches her eye. "I got this by falling off a skateboard when I was eight."

"Fucking *Lehna*," I mutter.

"What?"

"Nothing. So you weren't actually studying the trapeze, then?"

She laughs. "No. I did a lot of watching. It's so captivating. But it takes years to learn. Mostly, I was doing homework packets. Homeschool curriculum is . . . not the most stimulating unless you have parents who make it fun by, like, doing art projects and going on field trips and dissecting artichokes to discover they're flowers—"

"Artichokes are *not* flowers."

"Oh yes," she says, pointing her chopsticks at me. "They are." She pops an edamame bean into her mouth and grins. "I learned it from a packet."

I grin back at her. She's so confident, so effortlessly funny and smart.

"What about you, though? UCLA, right? So you must be into school."

I shrug. "I guess so. Mostly, I just really like art."

"It's crazy, isn't it?" she asks.

I cock my head.

"Finally meeting each other."

"Yes," I say.

"I only wish it wasn't so late. So close to when you'll leave, I mean."

I don't want to think about leaving for college. But now the thought is here, all around me, the heaviness of it, the way it pulls me under. I want to lose myself in Violet, but she's right across the table, not in a faraway place I can only reach in daydreams.

I feel panic rising, and I need to turn away from it.

"I got your rose," I say.

Surprise flashes across her face.

"How did you know about that?"

It feels so long ago now, even though it's only been a couple days. I call it all back: the way it felt to hang out with Mark that first night, how I discovered a new way friendship could feel. The song "Umbrella," my icy glass, the relief on Mark's face when I asked him to be my friend.

"I did go back to Shelbie's house that night. I was just too late. And Lehna told me that you had brought me a flower."

"But, still . . . ?"

"And June told me that you had left to see the sea lions, so Mark and I went to track you down. We thought we could catch you. We went to the pier and we walked all over, but no one was there. But then, there was a rose."

"Amazing," she says. "Talk about putting things out into the world."

"I'm sorry about that night."

She shrugs.

"Things happen," she says. But she sounds hurt, so I go on.

"I wanted to meet you so badly. And I got so nervous."

"What happens when you get nervous?"

"Why do you ask?"

"I want to know everything I can about you. I've been waiting and wondering for so long."

I try to think of a good answer, one worthy of so much patience. But all I can think of is the truth.

"I don't know," I say. "I guess I run away."

She locks eyes with me. A smile tugs at her mouth.

"I hope you aren't nervous now," she says.

* * *

Back outside, the fog is coming in and it feels less like summer.

"What now?" I ask her.

"I have to go to work."

I pull out my phone. It's almost seven.

"Your work starts now?"

"Yeah. Shelbie's mom got me a job with this woman she knows. She's divorced, has two kids, lives in a huge Pac Heights house. I go over after her kids finish dinner to help her do stuff."

"Like what?"

"Organize her receipts, place online orders, that kind of thing. She does a *lot* of shopping."

"I could walk with you?" I offer.

She smiles.

"I'd like that," she says.

She takes off her scarf. It glitters in the lowering sun. When she puts it back on, she wraps it in this elaborate way that covers most of her hair and sticks out, messily, on one side. She looks elegant and fearless.

"This way," she says, and leads us up a couple blocks before turning right on Fillmore.

"What are you going to do with all the paintings?" I ask her.

"I'll hang them up, of course! I have this tiny studio with bare walls."

"They aren't even very good."

"Oh, please."

"No, really. I thought they were okay before. But seeing them on the table like that, and then listening to Audra and Brad—"

"Fuck Audra and Brad. I've never encountered such ridiculous humans."

I laugh without thinking. Without meaning to. It comes out loud and sudden enough to make the people around us on the sidewalk glance in my direction. It feels so good, and Violet's so joyful, and I find myself wishing I could keep this moment forever—never go home, never back to school, never have to think about Lehna or worry about the future—just stay on this posh street with this brilliant, ravishing girl.

"Here's the thing about art, though," she says. "This may be an unpopular opinion, but it's what I came to believe after traveling for years with incredible artists who risk their lives to perform for audiences who don't care about who they are seeing, only that they are seeing a good show. True art is about creation. What's left after the creating is over is secondary. I checked your Instagram on my phone all the time when we were on the road. I saw the circus scenes and the stars. And yes, they were skillful, and the colors were amazing. But I loved them because they proved you were thinking of me."

She stops mid-block and grabs my hand.

"I didn't buy them because they were paintings, even though they *are* beautiful paintings," she says. "I bought them because, like Lars with his spray paint, you've been writing me love letters."

And then she is kissing me, right here on the sidewalk on a foggy summer night. Violet is kissing me, and everything is perfect. The kiss doesn't end. We are not two girls on a polite first date, bestowing a customary goodnight peck.

No.

We are kissing like girls who have ached for each other for years. Who never even spoke but somehow exchanged *I love yous* anyway. Who pored over photographs and gazed into computer screens and dreamed, over and over again, of this moment.

A clap begins; a whoop follows. More cheers, more applause.

"Happy Pride!" a voice yells, and then more voices join in.

If it were up to us, we'd keep kissing forever. But eventually, we have to let go. The strangers are kind; they don't stick around to make us self-conscious when it's over.

"I'm so glad I'll see you tomorrow night for the show," she says.

And I don't trust myself to speak, so I just nod, certain that my face conveys more than enough of my own gladness.

She says goodbye, and I lift my hand in a wave, and on the way back to my car I think of her kiss. I touch my fingers to my lips. I am tingling; I am love-drunk. On the road I hear her voice playing back all the incredible things she said tonight.

I want to tell Mark what happened.

I want to know what it would feel like to say the words, *Violet kissed me.*

I want to tell Lehna, too, but I don't know how I'd begin. And I don't know why she felt she had to lie to us about each other when the real Violet is everything I could wish for. As I pull onto my street, dread creeps in. I'm going to have to talk to Lehna sometime. Soon. But not tonight.

I turn into my driveway and cut off the Jeep's engine.

Just a few blocks away, Lehna is probably at her dinner table with her parents and her brother, oblivious to the fact that I've spent the evening with her cousin. Or maybe not. Maybe Violet is telling her right now. Maybe Lehna is checking to make sure she didn't miss a text from me, wondering why I didn't tell her first.

The night is dark now, the windows shining bright. My mom is in the kitchen washing dishes. She waves at me. I pretend not to see her.

I don't want to walk into my house. I don't want to walk into my room. I want to go back to Fillmore Street, to the sensation of Violet's body pressed close, to the sounds of celebration.

When I step out of the Jeep, the warmth of the night startles me. We said goodbye only an hour ago. We stood kissing only thirty miles from here. But now the air doesn't even feel the same. The old anxieties rush back. I shouldn't have gotten into UCLA's art program. I shouldn't have gotten into the AntlerThorn show. All of my Instagram followers are the result of one very strange and fleeting night, and when Violet finds out who I really am—how normal I am, how unexciting—she'll be so disappointed.

The truth settles, heavy in my stomach.

Violet kissed me.

But my life is still my life.

MARK

11

I take the train back from the city and walk from the station to Ryan's house. Exactly what we'd planned to do on Saturday night, before it got hijacked.

I've tried to text him to get some sense of what he wants. But he's not saying. I wonder if it's possible that my message actually got through. I wonder if it's possible that we're really going to have this conversation. I've gotten so used to being on the edge of it that I forgot there might be another side.

The closest I ever came was after we watched *Milk* about a month ago. He smuggled it onto his computer like it was porn. We had to wait until a night when his parents were out in order to watch it. Which was laughable—I really don't think they would care. But he did. He does.

We had done so many things together by that point, but

we'd never wept. Not like that. Not for all the things that could go wrong. Not for all of the good things that could come out of it anyway. When the movie was done, I wanted to take on the world. And there was a strong voice in my head saying, *How can you take on the world if you can't tell him how you feel?*

The words were right there. The words are always right there, only an inch away from being said. But he was at a slightly further distance than usual, lost in his reaction to the movie. So instead of talking about us, we talked about history, and about how this year we would get to Pride one way or another.

Now that week is here, and not in the way I thought it would be. I get to his front door and ring the bell even though I don't have to—I've walked in plenty of times without ringing first. But at this moment I want to be announced.

When Ryan opens the door, he's beaming. Openly giddy.

"Took you long enough!" he says. Then, without another word, he bounds off to his room. I call out a hello to his mom. She doesn't answer, so I guess she's not home.

We have the place to ourselves.

Still, Ryan closes the bedroom door behind me. He puts some indie band on the speakers and makes sure the song is wrapping around us. I kick off my shoes and sit on his bed, because that's what I always do.

"I have so much to tell you," he says. "So so much."

He can't stand still. He's changing the song. He's lining up my shoes. He's fiddling with a tennis racket that for some reason is on his desk.

"Okay," he says. "Where do I start?"

I see how happy he is. I see how eager he is to talk to me.

And I realize with a painful clarity that comes from years of studying his face: This has nothing to do with my message. This has nothing at all to do with us.

He doesn't sit down next to me. He stays by the desk, fiddling with the racket.

"So the thing is, Taylor is throwing a party tonight and he really, really, *really* wants me to come. It's not like a rager or anything—it's just a Pride thing his friends do. Watching movies and hanging out. It sounds so awesome. I mean, we've been texting so much it's like I already know most of the people who are going to be there. He's friends with so many artists—there's this one girl who's a puppeteer. Like, that's her life's work. How cool is that? And Taylor's cooking—did I tell you he cooks? He's not braggy about it or anything, but I have this sense that he's awesome at it, too. I mean, you don't make the food for your own party unless you're good, right?"

I don't even buy the potato chips for my own parties, so I can't begin to answer that question.

But Ryan's not looking for an answer. He just wants me to listen.

"I know it's last-minute, but I would love it if you could come with me. Taylor's really excited to meet you, and honestly I'm not sure I'm ready to go back and forth from the city solo. Taylor would've come and picked me up, but it's his party, so he has to do all the pre-party things. And like I said, some of his friends sound really cool, so who knows—maybe you'll hit it off with one of them. And even if you don't, we'll just be watching movies, so it's not like you'll be forced to have awkward conversations if you don't want to."

He is so blithely happy and I can't stand it. I honestly can't stand it.

He keeps talking. "I know it's not as exciting as the party you were at on Saturday night—which you still need to tell me all about, by the way. But yeah. It'll be fun. Really."

"So let me make sure I've got this right," I say. "You made me come back here from the city just so I could go back into the city with you?"

"I didn't know you were in the city until you told me you were on the train! I thought you were at home. Maybe working on your *Plath project*."

"What does that mean?"

"Why don't you tell me? I think you're the one with the secrets here."

He says it playfully, not meanly. He's in a good mood. He's having a ball. The world is his oyster, Taylor is his pearl, and I'm somewhere on the other side of the shell.

I want to play along. I want to be his friend here. I want to be able to smile and laugh and slap him on the back and go along with whatever he says.

But I can't. I just can't.

"No," I say.

Ryan looks at me strangely. "No?"

"Yeah. No."

"What do you mean, no?"

"I mean I can't do this. I really, truly can't do this."

My heart is in full panic mode. Of all the things I've imagined saying to him, why is this the one that's coming out? I'm already figuring out how to backpedal, how to pretend I'm only kidding. It's not too late.

Then he asks, "You can't do *what*?" And it's too late.

"Are you serious?" I say. "Can you possibly be serious?"

He puts down the tennis racket, as if doing this suddenly

makes him serious. He's looking at me like I'm a pet that's gone feral.

And, fuck it, maybe I am.

"Look," he says, "I'm sorry I yanked you back here to go into the city again. Had I known you were there, I would've just met you. You understand, right?"

"No," I say. "No no no no no no *no*. This isn't about that. You can't possibly think this is about that."

This is where he should ask, *Then what's it about?* But he doesn't. Because he knows. And asking that question will take us one step closer to the answer.

I give it to him anyway.

"When I say I can't do this anymore, I mean I can't continue to trample over my own feelings just to keep things okay with you. I can't. And that means I can't sit here on your bed and tell you that, sure, I would love to go with you to your new boyfriend's party. The fact that you could ask me to do that means you've done a much better job separating yourself than I have. But there's only one me, Ryan. And he's so fucking in love with you it's scary."

I'm starting to shake. I can't believe this is happening.

"He's not my boyfriend," Ryan says.

"*That's not my point!*" I shout.

"I know." Ryan's voice is quieter now. "I know that's not your point."

There. I've done it. I've defeated his good mood. And it doesn't make me feel any better.

"We talked about this," he says gently. "We knew what we were doing."

"We were lying!" I tell him. "The whole time, *we were lying.*"

He shakes his head. "I never lied to you."

"No, but you lied to yourself. If you actually feel there isn't anything more to what we're doing than friendship, or if you really don't think that fooling around affects what we are—then you're lying to yourself. But have you ever really believed it? Do you really have no idea how much I love you? How much I want this to work out?"

Ryan looks horrified, and I understand that both of us have been afraid of this conversation, for different reasons.

"Why are you doing this?" he asks.

"Because you are the best thing in my life and I know I'm the best thing in your life. Because it's one thing for me to think you aren't ready to be with anyone and it's totally another for you to want to be with someone besides me. Because I know how it feels when we kiss each other. Because I feel like I have spent my whole life waiting to tell you the truth, and if I hold it in any longer, it is going to make me hate both of us. Because I don't want to be your wingman—I want to be your goddamn copilot."

"But what if I don't want that?" Ryan is adamant. "What if I want Taylor?"

I can't look at him. I am falling apart. I wrap my arms around myself. I stare at the carpet under my feet.

"I mean," Ryan continues, "what if Taylor's the one I want to date? That doesn't mean I don't want you as my best friend. I want you as my best friend. Always. Doesn't that matter more than dating?"

I don't look up. "I know. I know all that. And maybe I'm being selfish, but I want everything. I want all of you. Because I'm in love with all of you."

I say this and I realize—there's nothing else I can say. I

can repeat it a million different ways—but there's nothing more I can add, nothing stronger than this.

I am trying not to think about kissing on this bed. I am trying not to think about being naked on this carpet. I am trying not to remember all the times we closed that door and became those people and made everything feel possible.

He walks over and sits next to me. I feel the weight of him against the mattress. The dip and the slight lift.

He puts a hand on my shoulder. Not romantic. Consoling.

"Look," he tells me, "I can say it over and over again. You are my best friend. You are my best friend. *You are my best friend*. I love you like that, which is huge. I don't want to hurt that, and I don't want to hurt you. I know you're making it seem like it's obvious that you'd react this way to Taylor, but honestly, it feels out of the blue to me. I know it isn't—I know that now. But you have to understand, to me it is. I never thought what we did was . . . that. I am very, very sorry if you did. But I didn't do anything to make you think that. I didn't. It's always been clear to me. And that doesn't make you any less awesome to me. You are completely awesome to me. You're just not my boyfriend. You're my best friend."

"But do those have to be two different things?" I ask, barely keeping the sob from engulfing my voice.

"In our case, yes."

This is so much worse than I feared it would be.

We sit there for a minute or two. I have nothing left to say. He has nothing left to say.

Finally, it's Ryan who breaks the silence.

"Look, I saw you dancing on that bar. And I read about your adventures on Saturday night. Man, that made me jealous. But I'm glad for it, because it shows that you're going to have plenty of opportunities—you're going to find someone as awesome as you, and I'm really hoping that when you do, you'll tell me all about it. Because that's what best friends do. And even though right now it's so totally awkward, I know it'll pass, and I know it'll be fine, and I know we'll get through this. Okay?"

I don't want someone else. I want you, I think. Even now.

But I'm back to keeping it inside. Before it was because I feared it wouldn't work. Now it's because I know it won't work.

I can't tell him it's all okay, either. I can't lie like that.

I just look at him and think all of the old things one more time.

You are so beautiful.

I understand you.

You understand me.

I know you well.

We're in this together.

We can be together.

We can cut through all the bullshit, and what we'll find underneath is love.

I know I should let go of all of these things—but you can't let go of something that's inside you. You're not holding it like that.

You are not good enough, Mark.

You will never be good enough.

How could you ever expect him to see you that way?

He was using you, and now he's done.

You were just a substitute until he found someone better.

And now he's found someone better.

Ryan stands up. Goes to his bookcase. Straightens something on the shelf.

"I'm sorry for dragging you back here. And for thinking it was a good idea to invite you to Taylor's party. I'm going to leave it up to you whether you want me to tell you about it or not. I'll understand if you don't want me to. I don't have to talk about him at all to you. Whatever it takes for us to get through this."

It would help if he were acting like more of an asshole. It would help if he would say the absolute wrong thing. That way I could storm out. It's too hard to just leave.

But he has a party to get to, and I have nothing left to say out loud. So I stand up. I find my breath. I force myself to meet his eye.

"I'll see you tomorrow," I tell him. And then, because I know I will hate myself for it, I add, "Have a good night."

"You too," he replies.

We're just so helpless.

I open the door. I decide not to look back.

"And, Mark?"

I look back.

"I would fight for you, too," he says. "I hope you know that."

I can't. I just can't.

I run away before I lose myself completely.

TUESDAY

Kate

12

I wake suddenly—warm summer light through my window—and check my phone.

Nothing.

Which is so strange, because Mark said he would text no matter what. Whether it was good news or bad news, *I love you* or *I love you not.*

So?? I write now, and then I carry the phone with me down the hall, set it on the edge of the sink. As I shower, I keep waiting for it to buzz. Maybe the water is too loud, or maybe, while I'm standing under it and thinking of kissing Violet, I am too swept up in the memory to listen closely. But when I draw the curtain and check again, he still hasn't answered.

I worry while drying my hair. I worry while applying mascara. I worry as I raise the tube of lipstick to my lips, but then I rethink the lipstick altogether. Violet and I are going to see each other again tonight, and I don't want to have to think about red smearing on my face or getting on her perfect mouth.

I don't want to think about anything.

When she kisses me, I will lose myself in it.

I keep my phone on my lap as I drive to school, a rare violation of the no-phones-in-the-front-seat rule that my parents set for themselves and for me. The three of us are prone to distraction and lost causes when it comes to patience. It's better not to tempt us. But the drive is textless, and as I park I decide that the night must have gone well for Mark.

Because if he is anything like Lehna or June or Uma, he wouldn't necessarily text me if he was deliriously happy, but he would absolutely text me if he was crushed. He would send me *novels* via text. Multivolume collections of sad poetry. I would be up all night typing *Oh no!* and *So tragic!* and *Want me to come over?*

The more I think about it I realize that not only did Mark's night go well, it must have gone *really* well. Like, stayed-up-all-night-together well. Passionate, *how-could-I-not-have-realized-before* well. Maybe they forgot to set their alarms and Ryan's parents discovered them this morning in a state of undressed togetherness and they are both being lectured to at this very moment. Or maybe that already happened late last night and now they are grounded and their phones have been confiscated, which explains why Mark hasn't texted me.

On the way to my locker I take a detour through the C hall where Mark's locker is, but there's no sign of him. No sign of Ryan, either. I'm on my way to my hall when two junior girls stop me.

"We can't wait for your show tonight," one of them says.

"Yeah," says the other. "I heard all your paintings already sold. That's so impressive. Congratulations!"

"Wow," I say. "Thanks."

With everything happening with Violet and Lehna and Mark, I haven't quite processed my new status in the spotlight. It is bewildering. And I can't exactly revel in it now, because if these girls I barely know are already privy to the information that someone bought all my paintings, Lehna must know, too.

But Lehna is actually nice to me when I get to our lockers.

"Big night," she says.

"And to think it all started as a lie," I say. "I keep waiting for something to go wrong. I don't think lies are meant to come true."

"It wasn't a lie. It was wishful thinking. Or magical thinking? Something like that."

I shrug. I don't know what it was to her, but to me it just felt like deception. Like trying to make myself into something greater than myself. And now I guess it's all come true, but I still feel less than worthy of this.

"So, I'm driving June and Uma tonight. I'd be happy to drive you, too. Like, in case you might want to have champagne? I heard there's usually champagne at these things. . . ."

"Oh," I say. "I haven't even thought about how I'll get there yet."

She nods, like it's casual, like this isn't a peace offering. Or a test.

"You can just let me know if you want me to pick you up." She clicks shut her lock and adds, "Even at the last minute."

"Thank you."

"No problem."

She smiles, about to walk away, but I don't want her to go. She's being so nice and I am so undeserving. There's so much I haven't told her about yesterday.

"Hey," I ask her. "Is Candace going?"

She nods and smiles.

"That's great. I really want to get to know her better."

"Violet's going to be there, too, you know," she says. "Are you going to be okay with that? It's a lot of pressure for one night. And we both know how you are under pressure."

I need to tell her, but the hall is almost empty. We're going to be late for class.

"Maybe we can talk at lunch," I say.

"Yeah, of course. See you then."

And then she strides past me toward her class, and I should be headed to mine, too. But instead I keep standing until the bell has rung and the doors along the corridor have shut and silence has descended. Until I am alone with myself.

Each period brings me closer to lunch and further from the certainty that Mark's day is being spent in post-hookup bliss. It didn't help that when I saw Ryan in the hall he told me he'd see me later at my show.

"AntlerThorn, right?" he said. "Ha."

"You know it."

"No, but, come on. *AntlerThorn?*"

"I don't get it. But wait, where's Mark?"

He didn't answer, just looked embarrassed and muttered something about getting back to the lit mag, even though we both know the last issue is finished and distributed and all that's left to do in that class is hang out.

I check my phone as soon as I'm back in the gym locker room after volleyball. Still nothing from Mark, but there's a message from a 415 number.

"Kate! Doll. I have good news and I have more good news disguised as bad news. First, your paintings are hung and they look just, how should I say it? *Quaint.* They are positively quaint. Now, the other piece of news might send you into a bit of a tizzy, but I promise you, there is nothing you can't pull off in two hours. You are a remarkable little girl. Here it goes: It slipped my mind yesterday that all of the members of this show donated a piece to be auctioned off for programming at the Angel Project. I figured you would donate a piece that didn't sell—because really, we never would have imagined that they would *all* sell—but then that collector girl surprised us! I had to pick my *jaw* up off the *floor*! And in the process I forgot all about the auction. We need a new piece from you and we need it before the show so it can be photographed for the online bidding. I have a courier scheduled to be in front of your school at two p.m. sharp. I know you can do this. Don't you dare let me down."

It's a nearly impossible undertaking, but it's also the perfect excuse to avoid Lehna. Instead of heading to the senior deck, I go to the art studio, thankful to find my teacher eating lunch in her classroom while browsing the Internet.

Have to spend lunch in the studio, I text Lehna. *Just found out I have to give another painting.*

Whaaat? she writes back. Because she knows better than anyone that my paintings take days. All the layers of paint that need to dry. All the details I like to add. All the colors I devote hours to mixing as I search for the perfect shade or hue. But as I set a blank canvas onto my easel and open the lid to my box of paints, I think about what Violet said. Art is about creation.

So I create.

I'm making good progress, working faster and looser than usual, not worried about getting anything right. But the lunch period is still too short. I call across the room to Ms. Gao. I tell her that it's an emergency. "Any chance you could get me out of Ms. Rivera's class?" Everyone knows that Ms. Gao and Ms. Rivera are friends. We've even seen pictures of them on Facebook in normal clothes, drinking cocktails on the weekends.

"I'll see what I can do."

She disappears and then comes back with her cell phone extended.

"Kate, I am so proud of you!" Ms. Rivera says. "Carrie—I mean Ms. Gao and I are totally going to your show tonight. Of course you can take this time to work on your painting! I'll announce your event to the class. Just review the last unit of the book before the final if you can. But you're already getting an A, so don't worry too much. But just review it in case. Okay, back to work for you!"

I dip my brush in red paint and put my headphones on as Art 2 kids fill the room. I try not to feel their stares.

It might be my best work, and it might be my worst. At two o'clock, I barely look at it. I find a cardboard box and set it inside and walk it out to the courier. I have felt the strange sensation of being the focus of the collective student body's gaze today already, and the fact that there is a black town car with a man standing in a suit outside of it holding a sign that reads KATE CLEARY doesn't exactly normalize things.

"Hey," I say.

"Good afternoon."

"So, um, the paint is still wet. So if you could just, you know . . ."

He takes the box from my hands. He looks inside.

"I can assure you that the utmost care will be taken," he says.

"Thank you."

"Is there anything else I can do for you at this time?" he asks.

Teach me how to talk to my best friend again, I want to say. *Keep me from fucking things up with the girl I've been waiting for. Tell me what to say to someone whose heart has been broken.* Because by now, I know that Mark is not being punished for having great sex last night. It was a nice theory, but the harsher truth has been seeping in and soon I'm going to have to face him and do my best to be the friend he needs me to be.

I may not know how to help myself, but I hope I'll know how to help him.

The courier waits in patient expectancy for my answer.

"Nothing," I say.

He nods. When he drives away, he takes the speed bumps in slow motion.

After a period spent feeling the emptiness of Mark's desk next to me, I look up directions to his house and then head over. He lives on the other side of town from me, in a modest ranch house similar to my own. Instead of the generic green lawn, it's expertly landscaped with succulents and flowers and vines.

As I walk up to the door, I pass a few Adirondack chairs around a tiled outdoor table with a cut-flower centerpiece.

I knock on the door. Wait. Ring the bell. Wait.

Desperate, I try the knob, and it opens.

So now I've let myself in, which I never would do under normal circumstances, and I make my way through the tastefully decorated living room and down the hall, in search of Mark's room. It isn't difficult to tell which is his: Only one of the doors is decorated with a baseball jersey.

I knock lightly.

"I'm trying to sleep!" he calls from the other side.

"It's Kate," I say.

He's quiet at first. Then, "Kate?"

I open the door. It's dark inside, so it takes me a moment to focus on him, curled on his bed.

"You found me," he says.

"Well, yeah, I was desperate. I've been trying to reach you all day." I sit next to him on the edge of the bed. "Way to keep a girl guessing."

He turns his face toward mine, and my breath catches.

I expected real sadness, but I did not expect this: His face is puffy with crying; his eyes are pink and swollen. I see none of his easy charm, or even his hurt or his worry.

I see no resemblance to the boy who has become my friend.

"I'm sorry I couldn't text."

"No," I say. "Please don't say you're sorry."

"I hid my phone in my hamper. I didn't want to know if he called me. Or if he didn't."

"That makes sense."

"Katie," he says.

"Yeah?"

"It was terrible."

I lift my hand from the bed. We haven't touched many times, but once I lower my hand onto his arm it feels right.

"I'm so sorry," I whisper. "It was our fault."

"It wasn't anybody's fault. It was only the truth."

"I didn't think it would go that way."

He's quiet for a long time.

"Neither did I," he says.

There's a window over his bed and I want to let the light in. He's still in his clothes from last night and he's all sweaty from crying.

"Have you eaten anything?"

"My mom made me breakfast."

"It almost four. You need something."

I head to the kitchen to make him a PB&J. On the way I pass the television and a case of his parents' DVDs, arranged in alphabetical order. I choose one at random. Before entering his room again, I check my phone. Brad texted me a picture of a flier with my name listed directly below Lin Chin's. *Post to Insta ASAP,* he's instructed. I think of her beautiful cranes, so delicate. I once read an interview with her where she described learning how to fold origami from her friend's mother. She said that they didn't speak the same language, so they spoke through the paper and the folds and the figures they created.

Then I think of my paintings next to her pieces, and my stomach drops.

I knock on Mark's doorframe and step into his room again. "I thought we could watch something," I say, handing him his sandwich.

He's sitting up now, running his hand through his bedhead.

"Your show," he says. "I can't believe I spaced. I need to get ready."

"The reception doesn't start until six thirty. We have time."

"But we should leave by five, then."

"I can be fashionably late."

"So we should leave at six."

"Or a little later."

Then I start to say something.

I stop myself.

And then I say it anyway:

"Or we can skip it."

As soon as I say it, relief washes over me. The relief is on Mark's tear-wrecked face, too, plain as anything.

"Are you serious?"

"Completely."

"I can't believe you would do that for me."

His gratitude is too much to accept, so I tell him, "I'm not only doing this for you." I have no business being in this show. How could I look Lin Chin in the eye and not die of embarrassment? How could I listen to Audra and Brad call my paintings quaint? How could I endure Lehna's glares from across the room? It would be so much easier not to go, but now is not the time to list all the reasons, so I say, "Holy fuck that place is hideous. Those walls!"

"It's a lot of pink."

"*Way* too much pink. So it's settled then. We can watch this movie."

"Are you sure about this?"

"Of course I'm sure. This movie stars Johnny Depp. You need to watch it to remind yourself that there are plenty of hot guys roaming the streets."

He looks pained.

"Only when you're ready for them," I add. "For now, they are in hibernation."

He smiles. I wasn't sure he'd ever smile again.

I head to his computer.

"Oh no," he says. "If we're going to watch this movie, we are going to *watch* it. Not squint at some dinky laptop screen."

So we go into the living room and watch on the giant flat screen as Johnny Depp's character falls in love with a strange girl from a bigger place. The whole movie is about how he wants to be somewhere else. Part of a different family. Part of a different town. Part of a different life. It seems like the girl might save him.

Violet.

I need to tell her I'm not coming.

But I don't even have her number. I could write her an email explaining, but I don't know how I'd begin.

It's past five now. Lehna is probably picking up June and Uma, checking her phone for my text accepting her ride or giving her a good reason why I'm passing it up. Instead she's getting silence.

And then it's six, and the movie is ending, and Mark and I are crying because it's a beautiful thing, how people can come together. There are so many ways to let people down, not nearly as many to get it right.

"Kate," he says, as the credits roll. "Explain this all to me. I mean, is this what you're usually like? Or is something going on?"

"What do you mean?" I ask, but it's just to buy time. I know what he means. The running away from every good thing. First from Violet and now from tonight.

"And I just realized," he adds. "All the other seniors I know talk about college constantly. I know you're going to UCLA, but only because you told my mother. You never talk about it, and you graduate in nine days."

I close my eyes.

Violet.

"Hold on," I say. "I just need to get my phone."

I take my time walking down the hallway. *You graduate in nine days. You graduate in nine days.* I'm getting light-headed; my hands are trembling.

I unzip my backpack and sit down on Mark's carpeted floor.

A text from Lehna: *Is this some kind of publicity stunt? Because you are nowhere close to being famous enough to pull that off.*

I type back: *I need Violet's number.*

A moment later, my phone buzzes: *Unbelievable.*

I wait to see if a number will follow, but it doesn't.

I don't know what I'll tell Mark when I get back to the living room. I could tell him the truth, I guess: that I worked hard on my paintings and sent in my portfolio. That I did so knowing that I wouldn't get in, because the art program is competitive and my work wouldn't stand out among the thousands of other applicants. But then I got the letter in the mail saying congratulations, and my parents cheered and my grandparents took us all out to dinner, and not a single time did anyone ask if this was what I really wanted.

Or I could give him the stock answer I've thought up for extended family members and friends of my parents: that I've heard the professors are amazing, that I'm looking forward to the beach and the sun and meeting new people.

Mark would see through that story. He would see through to me.

And the truth? The truth is that I don't think I deserve any of it.

Just as I reach the end of the hall, the front door opens and Mark's parents walk in, and I'm rescued by introductions and small talk about how Saturday night turned out. Then I hug Mark goodbye, hold him tightly around his neck. I want to tell him that I don't want to leave him. I want to know what he's going to do now. I want to hear about Ryan, and what exactly he said, and if there is still any chance of something between them.

But I really don't want to talk about me and how afraid I am.

I let go and I look him hard in the eyes. I don't know how much, if anything, his parents know about last night and I don't want to spill his secrets. So instead, since there is no chance of misinterpretation by anyone involved, I grab his face and I kiss him on the cheek.

"Mr. and Mrs. Rissi," I say. "I really love your son."

His parents beam, and Mark shakes his head, and I walk to my car.

When I get to my driveway I'm surprised to find the house dark, until I realize my parents are probably on their way to the city to catch the end of the reception after their days at work. I'll need to let them know I won't be there.

I turn to find my phone lit up with a text.

A single, short sentence from a number not in my contacts. I reach for it, bring it closer.

Make it up to me.

MARK

13

I don't want her to go.

There are about twenty minutes total while we're watching *Gilbert Grape* that I actually forget what's happening to me. Ryan has stepped out of the room and it's just me and Katie and the movie. My mind can relax. My body is comfortable. I am not a wreck.

But the movie ends and my parents come home and even though I don't want her to leave, Katie jumps away like she's finished babysitting and, no, she doesn't need my dad to drive her home. She kisses me on the cheek, tells my mom how great I am, and breezes away. I should be mad, maybe, but really I can't blame her. If I can't stand my own presence, how can I expect anyone else to? I'm grateful for the short forgetfulness she gifted me with I'm grateful that there was one person left in the world who knew I had to step out of it for a while.

Now here I am with my parents, and even though we're in our den and I'm back on the couch, it's like I'm stuck in the backseat on a long, long car ride, with my mom constantly scrutinizing me in the rearview mirror. I know I'm a mess. I know she notices. She notices everything. Especially messes.

But with my father here, she won't ask if anything is wrong. Because he'll tell her to butt out. His rough way of sticking up for me.

"I'm tired," I say, gathering myself together and making for the stairs.

"It's not late," my mother points out.

It is for me, I think.

I hope Katie's going to her opening. It was sweet of her to placate me instead of forcing me to go with her. I hope I haven't made her miss it.

I feel like a horrible friend for keeping her for so long, and for wishing she'd come back.

I dig my phone out from the bottom of my hamper, almost nostalgic for the person who wore the dirty clothes I'm throwing aside. I'm only getting the phone so I can wish her good luck.

But before I can do that, there's another text I have to see.

Are you okay?

How dare he ask me that. How dare he make it that easy. How dare he only ask it once.

I swore I wouldn't check my phone, and now that I've broken that vow it's like the other ones are null and void. Like any addict, I've built my floodgates out of tissue paper. In one strong rush, I am opening my laptop and checking every site or app where Ryan could have posted anything—I want to see how his night was, how his day was, how the story has gone on without me. I am Tom Fucking Sawyer (or is it Huckleberry Fucking Finn?) attending his own funeral, but I'm only fixated on the reaction of a single mourner. Except the mourner hasn't bothered to show up, because as I'm looking in window after window, there's not a word from him to be found, no image, no afterlife to be glimpsed. All I get on Facebook is that he's attending Katie's opening. It doesn't say whether or not he's plussed one.

I click on his list of friends. I type *Taylor* into the search box. Five people pop up. Two are girls named Taylor. Two are guys whose last names are Taylor. And one is the antichrist.

I know that's not fair. But it's not fair to see how pretty he looks in his profile picture, wearing a pink tank top in front of the Golden Gate Bridge, sunglasses tucked in the pocket over his heart, tattoos spelling out sentences that I don't dare zoom in to read. It's not fair to click on his profile and find that he plays water polo and has had poetry published in some Bay Area alternative weekly. It's not fair to see a post from 11:13 last night with a photo of Taylor with his tattooed arm around Ryan, sitting on a lime-green couch with two other guys, a feast spread out on a coffee table in front of them.

I wonder what time Ryan got home last night. If he got home.

Are you okay? No, I am not okay.

I am back on Ryan's page. There are no photos of Taylor in his timeline, but there are plenty of photos of us. Nothing remotely romantic to the outside eye. But I am seeing them with my inside eye, the one that knows that after the shirtless shot on the beach we went into the woods and kissed against a tree. The project we did on Krakatoa needed to be done in one night because we spent two weeks causing our own explosions instead of working on it. The snapshot of the two of us with our friends Lisa and Aimee after we watched *Frozen*—I know it looks like I'm leaning into him so I can be in the shot, but really I was leaning on him so I could put my arm around his waist, so I could hold him and feel my head angle into his. My inside eye sees the tenderness. My inside eye has been seeing these things all along.

My crying is so stupid. How does it actually help?

I should have told Katie more. Or maybe I should have thought about how this was a big night for her before I pulled her into the black hole my life has become. Only she didn't treat her big night like it was a big night. I don't know. My inside eye can't see beyond me and Ryan.

Which is also so stupid.

Are you okay?

Why is my phone back in my hand?

Why am I typing *NO* in capital letters?

Why am I hitting *send*?

This voice in my head says, *Get your shit together, boy.* But I'm confused. I don't recognize the voice. It's not Ryan. It's not me. It's like this military version of me. This serious guy with a deep voice. Why is he in my head? Does my mind honestly think I'll stop falling apart if it sounds like a drill sergeant?

I check my phone. Ryan hasn't replied.

It's been seven seconds.

I think about texting Katie and apologizing for taking up her time. Or thanking her for coming over. Or begging her to come back.

My mother's voice is somewhere in the air. It's calling me to dinner.

This is all my fault. For going into the city. For speaking up. For not leaving it alone. For forcing him.

I knew I would lose him if I said something.

I said something.

I lost him.

How can I blame him for that?

That knocking noise isn't in my head. It's my father at the door.

"You coming, kiddo?"

Ryan loved that my dad called me this. He would say, "If my dad called me kiddo, maybe I could tell him the truth."

He didn't mean about us. He meant about him. Which was tied to us.

I realize I haven't answered. My dad is waiting for an answer.

"I don't know," I tell him.

"You don't know if you're coming to dinner? Since your mother made it, I think a better answer would be 'yes.'"

That would have also been the better answer to *Are you okay?*

I check my phone.

"Mark." My father is getting impatient.

"I'm sorry," I say. I have no idea if I'm talking out loud or just saying it in my head.

What are you doing, Mark?

Okay, that one was definitely in my head.

You're acting like he's dumped you.

He hasn't dumped you.

In order to break up, you have to be together first.

"But we *were* together," I say. Out loud.

Luckily, my dad has already left the room.

I know I have to eat, and I know that my parents want me at dinner, and all of these obligations propel me to the kitchen, where my parents are already eating salad.

Ryan always thought it was funny that my parents started every meal with a salad. His parents weren't into vegetables.

I have no idea why I am thinking of them in past tense.

He is not dead.

He hasn't gone anywhere.

He even texted me to ask if I was okay.

(I check again. The phone will not leave my hand.)

"I hope Katie knows she could have stayed for dinner," my mother is saying. "I didn't get to talk to her much—but I like her."

"She had an opening to go to," I mumble defensively. I sound like she's accused me of chasing Katie away.

"Whose opening?" my father asks.

"Her own. At AntlerThorn."

My mother puts down her fork, even though there's still some lettuce speared on its tines. "What?"

"Her artwork is on display at this gallery. Tonight's the opening."

"Why aren't you there with her?"

Because I'm a shitty friend, Mom. And, incidentally, not worth dating.

"I don't know," I say.

She's standing up. Why is my mother standing up?

"Let's go," she tells me.

I don't understand what's happening.

My mother is looking up the address on her phone.

"I know where it is," I say.

And like that, it's settled.

As if he's some big gay bloodhound, Brad sniffs me out before I get through the door.

"Oh, thank God!" he cries, rushing over. "Audra was sharpening the pike for my head! And that's not the kind of head I like to give, ha-ha! Let me tell you, there's a fine line between fashionably late and fashionably *deceased*. And you do *not* cross that line with Audra. No, sir. But now that you're here, let me show you—"

Brad cuts himself off, because he's looked over my shoulder and found my mother, not Katie.

"Where is she?" he asks. "Please tell me she's parking the car."

"Who is this?" my mother asks. "Is he a *friend* of yours?"

The way she says *friend*, it's clear she means *special friend*. Like, *boyfriend*.

"It's so nice to meet you," she says, offering her hand to Brad. He checks out what she's wearing and approves.

"She's not parking the car," I murmur. Then I push into the gallery before Brad can throw more of a fit.

The space is barely recognizable from yesterday, because now it's packed with people. There are some faces from school, but mostly it's adults. Serious adults. Wearing serious jewelry. Having very serious conversations about Art. Or, at least, gossiping and making it sound like very serious conversations about Art. I am looking for Ryan and not finding him. Then I am looking for Katie and not finding her.

"You. Yeah, you."

I am not paying attention because I worry it will cost me too much. But when I feel a kick against my leg, I turn around and find Katie's friend Lehna. Her angry friend Lehna. Her other two friends are behind her. I feel awful, but I've forgotten their names.

"Where the hell is she? What the hell have you done with her?"

I ignore Lehna and look over to see my mom is still talking to Brad. From the way she's holding her purse, I think they're discussing where she got it.

Lehna kicks me again. "Focus, fratboy," she demands. "Katie has been acting weird ever since she met you. I want an explanation."

Do I want Ryan to be here? Why isn't Ryan here? Is he with Taylor?

Lehna is waving her hand in front of my face.

"Leave me alone," I say, and start to push toward Wall Six.

"Not so fast," Lehna says, grabbing my shirt. More people are watching us now.

Ryan is one of them.

Ryan.

I want him to look awful, but he doesn't look awful at all.

He doesn't look happy, either.

He looks checked out.

I cannot see him without it having an effect. I have never been able to look at him without having some kind of reaction. Happiness. Desire. Weakness.

Lehna is pulling harder.

I reach up and take her hand off my shirt.

"Don't touch me!" she yells.

I don't see Taylor. Ryan was talking to someone, but it wasn't Taylor. It was Anna from school.

Of course. Taylor wouldn't be here.

Taylor is still a secret. Because Ryan still has a secret.

I want to laugh. And at the same time, I start imagining punishment. It would be so easy. All I have to do is go up to him and kiss him. No. All I have to do is tell four gossipy people the truth. No. All I'd have to do is tell my mom, who will mention it to his mom. No. All I have to do is kiss him. All I want to do is kiss him.

Everyone will know. And if everyone knows, there will be no reason to hide. And if there's no reason to hide, there will be no reason to be apart.

I think Lehna is screaming at me. But that doesn't matter. I am walking his way and he is watching me walk over and I think, yes, I actually have the power here. All I have to do is kiss him in front of all these people. All I have to do is kiss him like it's the most natural thing, like practice has made perfect.

I love that he has no idea. As I'm getting closer, he has no idea. He is pretending that he doesn't feel anything. He is pretending that everything's okay. He is pretending that it is no big deal for me to walk across a crowded room for him after crying all day.

I am going to do it. I am going to show him. I am going to show everyone, and then it will be all right.

No. Don't.

That's Katie's voice. In my head. I stop, look around a second to find her. But she isn't there. She isn't one of the dozen people looking at me.

You found the weapon—now throw it away.

I am looking into Ryan's eyes and I know I am going to take that public kiss, that kiss that would have changed everything, and I am going to fold it up until it is too small to ever be found again.

Our eyes meet for a second. He looks sorry. Not happy. Not desiring.

Sorry.

"Where's Katie?" he asks.

And then Lehna is back in my face, back between me and Ryan. "You can't just walk away! Answer me!"

"I don't know where she is," I tell him, I tell her, I tell everyone. I don't mention that she was with me before. That's not theirs.

Ryan still looks sorry. He asked me because he didn't know what else to say. Now he's trying to think of the next thing. And because I was thinking so hard about kissing him, now all I'm feeling is the act of not kissing him, of having him here, but not really.

All of a sudden it's like the whole room is pressing on me. Lehna is angry and Ryan is blank and the constellations in Katie's paintings are spelling out a warning. I feel the two men behind me, kissing over all those years, and I see Audra cross like a hurricane over to my mother, and see Brad blow away from her, chastised. People are looking at me, but nobody's seeing me, and the pink walls are starting to waver in the corners of my vision, as if we're trapped in some crowded ventricle, some noisy heart.

I need a new life, and I need it right away.

I don't say goodbye to any of them. I push toward the valve, swim toward the door. I ignore every voice, every look, everything but my own thought to get out of here. I hit the sidewalk and turn left, go to the side of the gallery, the back of it. I sit down on the curb. I put my head down. I hold my head together.

There's a burst of incandescence, a rainless bolt of lightning. I look up into it, and when the blindness shifts back to seeing, I find Garrison, the photographer from that night, smiling down at me.

"Sorry about that," he says, lowering his camera. "But I couldn't resist. Such beautiful desolation."

"It's not beautiful," I tell him. "Desolation is *not* beautiful."

"It is from the outside."

"Well, I'm not on the outside."

He sits down next to me on the curb. "You will be one day. I know it doesn't feel like it right now, but someday you will be."

I'm not even sure he recognizes me—I can't see why he'd recognize me—until he asks, "So, did everyone like the other photograph? Did it have the desired effect?"

"Yeah, I guess," I say. "I mean, everyone was talking about it. Everyone but the guy I wanted the most to like it."

He pats me on the knee, in a way that Katie would, not in a way that someone at Happy Happy would.

"I can't believe I'm saying this, because I'm really not *that* much older than you. And I know that when I was your age, this kind of advice would have gone in one ear and out the other. But I'm gonna say it anyway. Most lives are long, and most pain is short. Hearts don't actually break; they always keep beating. This is not to diminish what you're going through, but I've been there, and I've been through it. As that famous homosexual Winston Churchill once said, if you find yourself heartbroken, keep walking."

"Winston Churchill was gay?"

"Well, no—I was just trying to add some levity there."

I can't say I feel much better. But I do feel a little calmer. So there's that.

The photographer stands. Raises his camera back to his eye.

"One more, for posterity."

I don't pose. I let him see me as I am.

"Imperfect," he says. "Which is perfect."

And then, like everyone else, he asks the question of the hour:

"Where's your friend?"

Kate

14

I find him on the sidewalk, exactly where his text said he would be.

"I can't believe you came," I say.

"I can't believe you didn't."

Even though we're behind the gallery, the lights and voices from within it tell me that the party is still going strong almost four hours after it began. I saw Ms. Rivera and Ms. Gao getting back into a car when I got here, but I can hear Lehna's voice and Brad's and a laugh so shrill and joyless it must be Audra's. I don't even listen for Violet's voice because I know Violet isn't here. She's somewhere else, waiting for me to make it up to her.

Brad's voice booms from inside, announcing one hour left to bid on the auction.

"Can we go somewhere else?" I ask. "We can come back here later, but I can't go in now."

Mark stands up.

I look at him; he looks at me.

We are not the same as we were on Sunday.

He runs a hand through his hair and even the way it falls has changed. He isn't a golden boy, charming a bar with his winsome looks and wholesome sex appeal. He's wounded and damaged, tired and lost. If he were dancing atop a bar now, just as many people would watch him, but not a single one would smile.

I can feel the change in me, too, but I don't want to think about it. It's one thing to be wrecked by another person, entirely something else to be wrecked by yourself.

"Garrison showed up here looking for you."

"Are you serious?"

"He took my picture and gave me advice. He may think he's my fairy godfather."

I smile in spite of myself, and then I think of Saturday night, of that mansion and all those people and the feeling that anything was possible.

"They aren't ever going to ask us what happened," I say. "If they haven't done it by now, they never will."

"I know."

The car parked in front of us rumbles to life, shines its headlights into my eyes.

"What advice did he give you?"

"Some stuff about hearts. And that Churchill quote about walking through hell, only he made it about heartbreak."

"Mr. Freeman loves that quote. Did you have him for history?"

"Yeah, sophomore year."

"I love his classroom. All of those nice posters he put in frames instead of just tacking them on the walls like all the other teachers do. How he always has tea on his desk and the electric kettle that makes the room all foggy when it's cold out. I never wanted that period to end. Even though we were talking about wars and betrayals and death, about all of these horrible things and how they repeat themselves, when I was in his room, everything somehow felt safe."

Mark is watching me as I'm saying this as though I'm answering his question from earlier tonight. And maybe I am. Or, at least, I'm doing my best considering that I don't know what the answer is.

What's going on with you?

If I could put it into words, it might not sneak up behind me like it does.

I close my eyes.

Violet.

But it isn't working anymore. She's no longer an idea or a spell or a daydream. She's someone whose mouth I've kissed. She knows I have issues and that I run away, and even though I should find comfort in the knowledge that she wants me anyway, I don't.

I can't find comfort anywhere.

"Let's walk," Mark says.

We pass the Japanese restaurant we went to with Violet. We pass a karaoke bar and a man laying out blankets in a doorway for shelter from the night, fast-food restaurants and a fancy jazz club, hipsters and beggars, a tattoo parlor and a church. And then the street becomes quieter, lined with apartment after apartment and no one but us and the rushing cars and the occasional person returning home.

We get to the end of a block and we stop. The city lights stretch below us.

Mark says, "I didn't even notice we were walking uphill."

"I didn't, either," I say, though I find that I'm catching my breath.

I'm trying to figure myself out. I keep failing.

"Tell me about that night," I say.

He turns to me.

"They aren't going to ask us, but it's still ours."

He nods.

"Okay," he says. "We showed up on the doorstep and we didn't know what to expect. We rang and waited for what felt like forever, but then that guy—George—he opened the door and he let us in. It was like a scene out of *Gatsby,* but gayer. Unless you agree with Mr. Chu and think that weird part with the ellipses means that Nick and Gatsby hooked up, in which case it was like a scene out of *Gatsby,* and just as gay. The place was full of ferns and overlapping rugs and champagne on silver trays carried by hot caterers and being drunk by even hotter guests. And George said, 'We've been waiting for you!' and even though it felt impossible, it also felt true." He takes a breath. "Now you."

"It was true. They *had* been waiting for us. We crossed under this giant chandelier to where the photographer was lounging with his friends. They asked us to tell them about our night, and everything we said, they loved."

"I can't believe how interested they were in us."

"I can," I say. I concentrate. I try to find the reason behind it. "What's happening to us—the decisions we're making and not making, the things we can control and the things that we can't—they are huge. And people can choose to forget how it was for them, or they can remember. They can half-listen to us and roll their eyes when we leave because we're young and we have no fucking clue what we're doing. Or they can actually listen, and they can think about themselves when they were like us, and maybe we can bring some pieces of them back." And now my eyes are welling up, my hands are trembling. "Because we *lose* it," I say. "We grow up and we *lose* ourselves. Sometimes when my favorite songs are on I have to stop what I'm doing and lie down on my carpet and just listen. I feel every word they're singing. Every note. And to think that in twenty years, or ten years, or five, even, I might hear those same songs and just, like, bob my head or something is horrible. Then I'm sure I'll think that I know more about life, but it isn't true. I'll know less."

Tears are covering my face now.

"Look at me," I say. "So stupid. You were probably expecting something real, but all I have to explain myself is some existential crisis."

"No," Mark says. "Don't say that."

"But really. Here you are, going through an actual event with Ryan, and here I am, freaking out because I'm thinking too much."

"No," he says again. "That's your future self talking. Your grown-up, dumb-fuck self."

I laugh. He reaches for my hand.

"Tell me what happened next."

"Okay," I say. "Let me think. Garrison's friends pulled out their phones and said they only needed ten minutes to make me famous. 'What's the gallery's name again?' they asked. 'What's your Instagram handle?' As they worked their magic, Garrison said he wanted to photograph us. He wanted to do it right there. He traded places with me so that I was on the sofa and he asked George—"

"—did we ever figure out who exactly George was? Like a young, hip butler? Are there even butlers anymore? Maybe a personal assistant?"

"I thought George lived there. Like he was one of the owners. He was so hospitable."

"Oh, crazy. Maybe he was."

"Anyway. He asked George to hand me a bottle of whiskey. I told him thanks, but I was driving. He said, 'I'm just asking that you hold it.' I said, 'I don't know how I feel about having a portrait taken of me holding a bottle of whiskey that I'm not even going to drink.' He said, 'It isn't in the frame.' And he had you look through his camera and you told me it was true. I guess it was supposed to make me feel something."

"Did it?"

"I don't know. Okay, yeah. Maybe it made me feel reckless."

"Do you think it came through in the picture?"

"I couldn't tell you. I've hardly looked at it."

"Why not?"

I shake my head. I can't find a reason.

"We can pick it up another time," he says. "Let's keep going."

Make it up to me. Make it up to me.

"What is it?" Mark asks. "You just stopped walking."

I guess I did.

"Violet," I say. "I don't know how I'll ever recover from

this. She bought all my paintings. People were probably asking her questions about them and me, and I left her there to guess."

"So call her," Mark says.

But I can't. I couldn't stand to hear the disappointment in her voice.

"Text her, at least."

"What do I say?"

"Ask her where she is. Go wherever she says."

"But I look like shit."

"You look beautiful. Go. Sweep her off her feet."

Violet, I text. *I'm so sorry. Where are you?*

The dots appear immediately. Then they stop. Then they're back.

Just got home.

"She's home," I say. "I don't know where that is."

"Ask her for the address."

I do.

I hold my breath.

She gives it me.

"It's in Hayes."

"That's close," Mark says. "Let's go."

I wish I could buy her a gift, but all the shops are closed, so when we show up at her house ten minutes later I'm empty-handed.

"Do you want me to wait for you?" Mark asks.

"Are you kidding?" I say. "You're coming with me."

"*Ummm*," he says, shaking his head. "That is *not* very romantic. Don't worry. I won't leave you until you tell me to go."

I nod, and enter the gate alone. I follow the instructions she sent in her text and round the house to the back, where there's a small studio, lit up in the night. I knock on the door.

She opens it.

It breaks my heart to see her. She's still dressed for the party in herringbone pants and high heels, a skinny black tie around her slender neck. If I saw her on the street I would stop still in lust and wonder.

But seeing her now, as she steps back to let me into her room, is too much for me to take. I look at her walls instead. They're mostly bare save for some black-and-white photographs pinned to one of them. I step closer. They're all of the circus.

"Did your mom take these?" I ask her.

She nods.

Her laptop is open on her bed, a YouTube video paused on the image of a trapeze artist in silver against a black backdrop, dangling from the bar by one leg.

I came to apologize, to confess. I did worse than desert her. I didn't even show up.

But instead I ask, "Do you miss it? The circus?"

She's quiet. I finally look at her for the first time since walking into her room.

"I thought I wanted to stay in one place," she finally says. "Make a life for myself here. But I can't even bring myself to unpack."

She gestures to her suitcase and her boxes and I see what she means. There is no dresser or desk or chair. Only a bed and a kitchenette without pots or pans or other signs of living.

"I'm not used to staying anywhere very long. I came here because I thought something might be waiting for me." She looks on the verge of tears, but she blinks them away. "Let's go out. I need some air."

"Okay," I say. "I should tell you that Mark's out front, though. In case you wanted to talk. I can tell him we need some time. . . ."

"To be honest," she says. "I don't feel much like talking."

I follow her outside, my throat tight, my eyes burning.

"Hey, Mark," she says. "I'm in a shitty mood. I think we should all get ice cream."

"I like ice cream," Mark says, and we walk, Violet leading us toward the heart of the neighborhood where ultracool adults laugh on street corners and sip from pint glasses in a beer garden. We are the only teenagers in sight.

I see the ice-cream store in the distance, but before we get there Violet stops short in front of a woman, sitting on a blanket on the ground.

"New plan," she says to us. And then to the woman, "I'm buying my friends readings."

I step closer and see that a sign on the blanket says *Tarot*.

"I'm not sure about this," I say.

"Yeah . . ." Mark cocks his head. "Thanks, Violet, but—"

"Admit it," Violet says. "You could both use a little clarity in your lives."

And even though I have done enough soul-searching for the night, I know that I can't let Violet down again, so I grab Mark's hand and lead him over. Up close, the Tarot reader's younger than I thought she'd be. Her blanket is soft under my legs and small enough that my knee touches Mark's.

"I'm Kylie," she says. "Have either of you had your cards read before?"

Mark and I shake our heads.

"A good way to begin is with a spread of three cards. The past, the present, the future. Which one of you wants to go first?"

"Him," I say.

"Oh, I don't think so," Violet says from behind us. Then, to Kylie, "Kate has a little problem with follow-through."

Kylie nods as though she already knows. She takes my hands in hers and I can't help but blush, and for the first time tonight I feel the cold of the evening, and wish I had brought a sweater or a jacket or at least a scarf, something to wrap around myself.

She lets me go and reaches for her cards but then stops.

She shifts to face Mark straight on and takes his hands. She inhales for longer than I knew was possible, and then exhales just as slowly.

"I'm going to do a joint reading," she says.

I glance at Mark. He shrugs. I wait to hear why, but all she says is, "It feels right."

She opens a gold box and pulls out her deck of cards.

"You shuffle," she says to me. And then, to Mark, "You cut."

He does. The fortune teller focuses.

"As I'm turning this first card, I already feel pain," she says.

I would like to keep an open mind, but we are two tear-stained teenagers. *Three,* if you count Violet. It doesn't take intuition to see that.

She reveals a beautiful card: a naked, joyful woman floating in the sky, surrounded by a green wreath.

"Oh yeah," she says. "*Man.* This card is the World."

"I don't get it," Mark says. "It looks like good news."

But the card, though beautiful, fills me with sadness.

"It's upside down," I say.

She nods.

"A reversed World," she says. "No closure. Too much left unsaid and undone. You know, I'm feeling this card pulling me toward you, Kate."

She looks at me.

"You've been holding yourself back."

My throat tightens in hurt but then anger.

"Yeah, well, you were just told that I lack follow-through."

She doesn't respond.

"Okay," I say. "So what am I supposed to do about it?"

She turns another card over. This time, a woman is blindfolded and tied up, with swords all around her.

"This is as clear as it gets," she says. "You're both hurting. You feel stuck." She turns to Mark. "Your heart"—she holds her hand to her own—"is broken, and you don't know how to move past it."

Mark shoots me a skeptical glance and I have to agree. Heartbreak is an easy assumption to make about a teenage boy with straight teeth and nice clothing but a look of desperation.

"She is someone you've been close to for a long time," she says. "I can tell by how deep the pain is."

I'm confused, but then Mark's smirk clarifies it: Kylie is just a woman in a costume, talking to a random boy about his love for a girl. She probably does this between semesters to make tuition money.

"Both of you, look closely," she says. "This figure is bound and blindfolded. She appears trapped, but she isn't."

"She's surrounded by swords," Mark says. "It definitely seems like she's trapped."

"But look. The swords don't go all the way around her, and only her arms are bound. If she would only trust herself to step forward, she would make it through. This card is a warning to you both. You can't allow yourselves to be trapped by your pain."

"Right," I say. "If you find yourself in hell, keep walking. That seems to be the theme of the night."

She says, "Could be. Or maybe, if you think you're in hell, open your eyes. What you see may surprise you."

She touches the last card, about to turn it over.

"This one will tell us about your future. Are you ready?"

We nod.

And she flips it over. Even though I don't really believe in this, even though Kylie is just a pretty girl telling stories, playing a game with our lives, fear grips me.

On the card is a tower struck by lightning, raining fire into a black sky. Two men are diving out to escape the flames, plummeting to the rocky ground below. I was expecting a card about strength or peace, Kylie quoting everybody's favorite words of encouragement: *Yes, times are hard now, but you'll find your way.* Instead I'm face-to-face with disaster.

"Okay," she says. "The Tower. This is a powerful card."

"Yeah," Mark says. "I can see that." His voice is shaking.

"Don't be scared," she says. "Or, okay, go ahead: Be scared. That's okay, too. Give me a second. Let me think."

She goes back to the beginning—our upside-down World—follows it to the Eight of Swords and then to the Tower again.

"I'm new at this," she says. "And I can see how these cards look frightening. They *are* frightening. But look at you two. You look horrible. You look sad and scared. You don't need the cards to tell you that. So if we follow the journey they are showing us, we can see that the tower is necessary. Something profound needs to happen. Something needs to change, and it is going to change *soon*. You may already know what's coming. It's going to shake you. It's going to change your world. But after the tower burns to the ground, and you've picked yourselves up off the rocks, and the fire ends and the night passes, it's going to be morning again.

"Mark," she says. "You think you are alone, but someone is on the horizon. I see love, *mutual* love, in your near future. It's not coming directly from the card, but it's a feeling I'm getting. It's someone you know but wouldn't expect. She isn't who you think she is. And Kate, that woman in the blindfold? She is you. But look at how her feet aren't even touching the ground. You are so close to being free."

"That's what I'm afraid of," I say.

"I know," she says. "I know. But change takes courage."

She sits back, as though she's finished, but then she leans forward again and stares at the cards.

"A thought is coming," she says.

We wait.

And then her face lights up.

"*He*," she says to Mark. "I'm sorry—I just assumed. I wasn't hearing clearly enough. *He* isn't who you think he is."

Violet gives the woman fifteen bucks and Mark stands up, but it takes me a moment longer to gather myself. Finally, I do. I try to call back my skepticism, but I can't muster it. Whatever this just was, it feels real, and when I turn around I can see that it's real for Violet as well.

She's staring at me, her sadness intensified.

"It sounds like you have some things to figure out," she says. "I don't want to get in the way of them."

I should tell her she has it wrong. I should lie and claim I don't believe in any of it. I should say, *Even if I did believe it, you could never be in my way.* I want to go back to her studio, to the moment when she said she thought something was waiting for her here. *I was,* I should be telling her. *I still am.*

But I take too long to say anything, and she gives my silence meaning. She nods. She forces the saddest smile.

"Let me know when you've figured it out," she says, and then she turns from us and walks back toward home.

WEDNESDAY

MARK

15

"Do you think it's him?" I ask, for the eleventh time in five minutes.

It's before school the next morning. We're sitting on the hood of Katie's car, sipping coffee and watching the boys head into school.

"Mackenzie Whittaker?"

"I'll bet behind that rough-and-tumble science-fair exterior, he's a kitten. Not at all who I think he is."

"What would the two of you talk about?"

"Science. We'd talk about science. Hot and heavy science. *Earth* science."

"How about him?"

She's nodding toward Ted Lee, a guy on my baseball team.

"Straight."

"You sure?"

"*Straight.*"

"You've given this some thought, haven't you?"

"Yes," I admit. "I've given this some thought. Some of the thoughts were pretty detailed. But the answer remains the same. He's straight."

"I hate that word. *Straight.* At the very least, those of us who are nonstraight should get to be called *curvy*. Or *scenic*. Actually, I like that: 'Do you think she's straight?' 'Oh no. She's *scenic*.'"

"You know what I hate?"

"What?"

I glance at Ted, who's looking really good. "I hate that we start everything with this qualifying round. Is he or isn't he? If I was into girls, I wouldn't have that. I'd just be able to go for it, since the odds would be in my favor. And if the girl happened to be scenic, it would just be, like, *oops*."

"But what if the guy you think is straight is *not who you think he is*." Katie says this as if she's in fortune-teller-training school.

"You know," I say, leaning back on her front windshield and taking a sip of coffee, "we need to have our own morning show. Just you and me on the hood of a car, talking about everyone who passes by. It could be massive."

"How about Diego? He's *scenic*."

Even though I know who she's talking about, I raise my eyes in his direction. Then I regret it, because he sees, and an awkward moment passes before he looks away.

"Oh," Katie says. "Interesting."

"He had a crush on me," I explain. "Like, for a while. Most of this year. He asked me out. Three times."

"And why did you say no? He's awesome."

"Because I was seeing someone else. Only, I couldn't tell Diego I was seeing someone else. So I didn't have a choice. I assholed him."

"You *what*?"

"I put up a total asshole front. I blew him off. I pretended he wasn't asking what he was asking. I made it seem like I was a conceited jerk, so he wouldn't think there was anything wrong with him. I tried so hard to keep him in the friend-zone. You have no idea."

I don't tell her he cried. That wouldn't be fair. But he did. The third time was the worst. *I don't understand,* he kept saying. And what could I do? *I just want you as a friend,* over and over until even I was having a hard time understanding it. Say anything enough times and it's only words.

"I'm sorry," Katie says.

"Not your fault."

"Not your fault, either."

"But it is, isn't it?"

"And Ryan's. Indirectly Ryan's."

"But he never asked me to do that, you know? I think he would have been happy if I'd gone out with Diego. He would've been thrilled. And it would have killed me, to see him that happy for that reason."

Katie does some math in her head. "So the whole time you've been with Ryan, there hasn't been anybody else?"

"There hasn't been anybody else ever. He's it. My only. How about you?"

"You know that stereotype that lesbians get married after the first date?"

"Is that a stereotype?"

"Committed to commitment—that's us. Only I seem to be the control to that experiment with my placebo heart. I rarely make it through the first date. The first half hour, maybe. Then . . . I just don't like them much. And I don't like me very much when I'm trying to impress them. So I stop. Escape when I can. And, of course, long painfully for the one girl I can't have."

"Until, of course, she leaves the circus and comes to town."

"Something like that."

We sit there silent for a moment. I'm sure Katie's thinking about the way the night ended, and I'm not sure I want to speculate about boys anymore. Because it raises the whole question of what I'd do if I actually found the right one.

"Look!" Katie says. "Here comes a very special guest! My ex!"

It's Quinn Ross who's walking over—Quinn Ross, Ryan's big poetry rival and the editor of our school's "underground" literary magazine.

"You dated Quinn Ross?"

"Yes. In third grade. For two weeks. It turned us both gay."

"Hey, Katiegirl," Quinn sings when he gets to us. "And hello, Markus-oh-really-us. School is wrapping up, and you two look like you're laying it down. I'm sorry I didn't make it to your gallery thing last night—I've been volunteering down at The Angel Project in the Castro. It's a pretty big week for us, fundraising-wise. Let all the people come and party for Pride—when they leave, there will still be homeless teens, and they'll still need help. Hey—you should come tonight. I'm hosting a poetry slam."

"Maybe," Katie hedges. "There are a few things we have to attend to first."

I'm hoping this means she's going to see Violet. But I don't say anything with Quinn there. He is an ex, after all.

"Well, I hope to see you at the slam," he tells Katie. Then he turns to me and says, "And I *really* hope to see you."

"Um . . . sure?" I say.

Quinn laughs to himself and walks away.

"I'm not sure I like your exes," I tell Katie.

"Quinn? He's harmless. All snark and no bite." She looks down at her phone. "I hate to say it, but we should probably head in. It would be lame to fail out in June because of attendance."

"Are you going to call her?" I ask.

"Yes. No. One of the two."

"Promise me. By the time we meet back here after school, you'll have communicated with her in some way."

"No. I can't promise you. Because I don't want to break any promise I make to you, and I'm not really sure that's a promise I can keep."

"You should call her. You should try to explain."

"I know. I will. Unless she doesn't want to talk. I wouldn't blame her for that."

"No, but you'll blame yourself."

She slides off the car. Gets her bag from the backseat. Says "I know" one more time, then heads off into school.

Ryan finds me right before lunch.

"This isn't cool," he says.

I'm at my locker. Caught.

"What isn't cool?" I ask dumbly.

"The silent treatment. The look of terror on your face right now. The way you're acting like this is all my fault."

"I never said it was all your fault."

"You might as well have." He stops, stares down at the floor, then stares back up at me. "You disappeared last night."

"I was right out back. If you'd looked for me, you would have found me."

"But you didn't want me to look for you, did you?"

Now it's my turn to stare down at the floor, be honest. "No."

"Exactly. Not cool."

He stops, and I know it's because people are passing us in the hall. People who could hear.

When it's safe, he goes on. "I saw you talking to Quinn this morning. That was a bit of a surprise."

"It was nothing. He's Katie's ex."

"Well, I'm sure he told you about his poetry slam thing." He pulls a flier out of his pocket and unfolds it. *Queer Youth Speak Out*, it says at the top. "Not very subtle. They even printed it out on pink paper, just in case you didn't pick up on the fact that it was gay." He holds it to his nose and inhales. "Mmm . . . smells like Whitman."

"Are you going?"

"Yeah, I think so."

"Are you going to read?" I ask, even though I know the answer's going to be no. Ryan's gay poems live in a very private place.

"Maybe."

Oh. "Maybe?"

"What may be, may be." He smiles. "You'll just have to show up and see."

What is he telling me? I don't know what he's telling me.

"Taylor will be there, and I think some of his friends are

going to be there. You should join us. If I go through with it, I want my cheering section to be bigger than Quinn's."

I want to be in control. I don't want him to see what I'm really feeling. But my walls aren't that high when it comes to him. The truth flies right over.

"Well, if Taylor's going to be there, you don't really need me, do you?" I spit out.

And Ryan's walls must be low, too, because he grabs my arm, right there in the hall, right where anyone could turn the corner and see.

"I'm only going to say this to you once, okay? I like Taylor. I'm excited about Taylor. I may want to date Taylor, if everything goes well. But I have known Taylor for a total of about five seconds, while I have known you since the mountains were made and the rivers were formed. I know we're in a weird place right now, but I want you to step out of it and be there for me. Taylor is a boy, and you are my best friend. Taylor is a date, and you are my calendar. Understood?"

I know I should say I understand. I know I should understand. But there's still a part of me that hates how easy it is for him to say these things. He wants to put it in perspective, but it's all his perspective.

Also, I don't want to be a best friend if I can't also be a boy in his eyes. I don't want to be a calendar if I'll never get a date.

"Are you really going to read?" I ask him. "In public?"

He smiles. "You can be such an Oblivious Oliver. Like I said, you'll just have to *show up and see.* Maybe you're not the only one who can dance on the bar—so to speak."

He's got me, and he knows enough to leave before he loses me. The result is a locker-side muddle. I don't have any desire to follow him into lunch, so I detour to the library again. I see

Dave Hughes sitting at his table by himself. He spots me coming and clears a space.

"Are you always here at lunch?" I ask after I sit down.

"Nah. This is actually my study hall. I have third lunch."

"Got it."

I see he's got the sports section on the table, and he nods that I can take it. Then he goes back to whatever he's doing on his laptop.

About five minutes later, I hear something that sounds like a *Pssst*. I ignore it, but it happens again. I look up.

"*Pssst*."

Dave's eyes don't leave his laptop, but he tells me, "It's coming from a girl in the shelves over there."

All I can see is a hand, its index finger indexing me to come over.

I don't recognize the hand, but when I step into the shelf area, I recognize the face of Katie's friend June.

"We never talked, we never saw each other, this never happened, okay?" she starts.

"Sure."

"If Lehna catches me, it'll be bad. She's like that. But I'm not taking sides. I'm really not. I don't want there to be sides, you know? It's not like anyone asked me—it's not like anyone said, 'Hey, do you mind if we divide into sides?' Because you know what sucks? Having friends who aren't being good friends to each other. That really sucks. And I know I should be talking to Kate, but if I talk to Kate, that will be taking sides, so I'm going to talk to you instead, and if you end up talking to Kate, that's not really my fault, is it?"

"No," I say. "Not at all."

"Good. Because Kate needs to be careful. Very careful.

Lehna's really mad. And at first it was just Lehna being dramatic, but now the reason is serious, because Lehna thinks that Kate's playing with Violet. Like, *really* playing with her. We all saw Violet at the art thing last night, and Violet was like, 'What's Kate's deal?' And Lehna was like, 'What did she do to you?' Violet said Kate stood her up and was being deluded—no, it wasn't that. Not deluded. The word that means hard to get. She said Kate was being that, and while she understood everything was like, wow, sudden, she's not going to wait around forever for Kate to focus. And Lehna—ohmygod, Lehna. Lehna was like, 'She's not worth it if she's going to do that to you.' And she's right, right, because no one should treat you like that. But she's also wrong, because it's Kate we're talking about, and we all know Kate's only acting like this because she's afraid. Or at least I think we all know that. It just stops being a good excuse after a while. And what I'm trying to say is, the time it stops being a good excuse? Well, that's now. Lehna's already sure of it. And Violet's getting there. So you have to tell Kate to do something. Really do something."

"But I *have* told her to do something. Just this morning."

June locks me into a look there, and it's like finding out that Hello Kitty doesn't have a mouth because *she can beam words directly into your mind.* "Well, try harder," she says. "We're all going to the Exploratorium this afternoon—if you and Kate come, I can make sure Lehna's distracted so Kate and Violet can talk alone. This is it—her last last chance. Give me your number."

I tell June my number and she enters it into her phone. Then she calls me so I can have hers.

"There," she says. "Remember: We never had this conversation."

"You're not taking sides."

"Right. I just want all my friends to be happy. And sometimes you have to do that one friend at a time."

I'm aware that I should contrive a reason for me and Katie to go to the Exploratorium—it's a fun place, so it wouldn't be too hard to say I need the pick-me-up that playing around at an interactive science museum can bring. And then, surprise!, we'll bump into Violet there.

A trick. I could easily trick her into going.

But I don't want our friendship to be like that.

So instead I sit down next to her at the start of math class and say, "I know where Violet's going to be this afternoon, and I think we should go there."

Kate sighs. "How do you know this information?"

"A little bird told me. And I'm not going to tell you anything more than that. I promised."

Katie nods.

I go on. "Also, I found out Ryan's going to be at Quinn's poetry thing." I tell her about the conversation Ryan and I had, and how weird it made me feel.

"So do you want to go?" Katie asks after I'm done. "Do you think he'll read?"

"I don't know. And I don't know. What about you? Do you want to go to the Exploratorium?"

Our teacher is clearing his throat, waiting for us to settle down so he can start.

"Let me get back to you on that," Katie says.

We make it through class. It's the end of the year; there's

no real reason to pay attention except to be polite to the teacher as he goes through the motions.

As soon as the end bell rings, I turn to Katie for an answer.

"Yes," she says. "But only because it's the Exploratorium."

I went to the Exploratorium so many times with my parents and on field trips as a kid, but the last time I went was with Ryan.

It was one of our first city excursions alone, and for two hours I wasn't worrying if we were boyfriends or best friends, or if someone was going to see us, or if this was the moment it would all click into place. No—for two hours, we got to be kids, running around and playing. We got to fool around with sound waves and pulleys. We got to pixelate ourselves and dance as a projector turned us into shadows on a kaleidoscope-colored screen. At the end of an exhibit about artwork created in a nineteenth-century mental asylum, we waded through the comment box and found a comment card written by a young kid: *I have lost my turtle. His name is Charles.* For weeks after, we pretended to be looking for Charles.

"He couldn't have gotten that far," I'd say.

"Maybe we should try the Shell station," Ryan would say back.

Eventually we forgot about Charles and moved on to other inside jokes, other references to what we'd shared and continued to share.

Charles is still out there, I'm thinking now. *He must be entering his awkward teenage mutant ninja years by now.*

I don't turn to Ryan and say this, because it's not Ryan

who's with me. It's Katie, and she'd have no idea what I was talking about. I could explain it to her, but it wouldn't be the same.

I feel like I've lost half of all the stories I know.

I hear Katie take a deep breath; we're about to reach the door. I'm not going to ask her if she's sure she wants to do this, because I don't want to give her a chance to say no.

I text June to let her know we're here.

I get a text back almost instantly.

Meet Violet by the mirrors.

Kate

16

I can't find the mirrors.

I've checked the little paper map, but there's so much to discover in here that it's practically useless. Mark told me he'd wait for me in the shadow room. He said he'd be in there for a while, in case I needed him, and if I didn't come back for him that would be a fine thing. A *good* thing.

"Just—don't forget about the poetry slam, okay?"

"Yeah."

"I really need you there."

"I'll be there."

"Okay. I'll be in here for a while, I think. My shadow has infinite potential."

The clock in the room started counting down and he rushed in. I saw him leap up, arm extended like he was catching a fly ball, and the light flashed bright and went dark again.

And now I'm making my way through the wings, looking for the mirrors. There are children and adults, tourists and members, and they are all playing. They're all engaged or at ease and I wish I could join them, but I need to find her.

I don't know what I'm going to say yet. I don't know what I'll do. But what I *do* know is that Kylie's voice has been in my head since last night and that she's right. I'm the one holding myself back. I'm the one who can make everything change.

I walk past people pressing buttons as fast as they can, watching numbers grow on a screen above them. Past a guy staring at his own reflection. Past people wearing headphones and a group of kids holding magnets over a huge table. And then I stop short because I see Lehna and June and Uma. Lehna's back is turned—thank God—but June sees me and her eyes go wide. Slowly, she lifts a hand to her side and points me down the hallway. I nod a silent thanks and head into the center of a group of tourists to pass them.

And there, finally, is Violet in front of a giant mirror. Her reflection is upside-down. As I walk closer to her, I appear there, too.

She smiles an upside-down smile.

I frown an upside-down frown.

Not at her, at myself, at the way I've been acting.

My phone buzzes in my pocket. It's June.

Quick! We're heading in your direction! Trying to stall!

So I grab Violet's hand and I lead her away from there, out of the wing of the museum that's about sounds and light and into a greener space where the air feels cooler. All around us are giant tanks full of starfish and coral and anemones, and overturned trees with their roots in the air, and the greenest plants.

I let go of her, but she grabs my hands.

"Why are you here?" she asks me.

"To see you," I say.

"But last night," she says. "When I gave you an out, you took it. You've been so elusive."

"You're right," I say.

"Why?" she asks. I open my mouth to answer, but she says, "Don't answer yet. Let me tell you why I'm asking."

I nod, knees weak. Even being silenced by Violet is amazing. Even being told difficult things is, and I know what she's about to say is going to be difficult by the way she's unsmiling, by the crease between her perfect eyebrows, by how she looks away to decide which words to start with.

Whatever she says to me—I will deserve it. If she calls me fickle, I'll know why. If she says she can't do this, I'll understand. But it might crush me.

"I'm asking," she says. "Because I don't *want* elusive."

She shakes her head. There are tears in her eyes, and I see how I've hurt her. How much better than this she deserves.

"I put myself out there for you," she says. "I got you a rose, but you didn't let me give it to you. I showed up at that gallery just to see your paintings, and then I saw something even better—I saw *you*. We got to meet. Finally! And you were everything I wanted you to be. And then I bought your paintings! I was so reckless, which really isn't like me, but I wanted to do something grand. I wanted to sweep you off your feet. And then laughing in the streets with you and Mark. Talking at dinner. That walk. That *kiss* . . ."

I try to speak again, but she shakes her head.

"I'm not finished," she says. "I don't want elusive. Remember Lars and his poem? I want a love like that. I want pure and true. I want it with you. Even though this might sound crazy, it's part of why I came back. We never even texted or talked, but I thought we had a connection anyway, and I thought I might find that kind of love with you. But if you don't want it—if *this* is how you are, always running away or just not showing up, if it turns out that I'm not who you thought I was going to be—then I'm going to get it with someone else."

There are tears on her cheeks now, but she's shrugging, letting me know that she'll be okay moving on. And of course she would be. I mean, *look* at her. She could find someone new to love just by walking down the street.

"Okay," she says. "I'm done now."

"Okay," I say. "I'm starting."

I breathe deep. I look into her eyes. I wish I could take her face in my hands and kiss her, but I know she needs more than that right now. Even though I want to give her everything, I've learned enough in the last few days to only promise what I know I can deliver.

"I don't want to let you down again," I say. "I don't want to be elusive. Last night, I was skeptical when you bought me that reading, but everything Kylie said made sense. All night long, all day today, I've been seeing those cards and wondering what they mean for me. I *know* that I'm holding myself back. I know that something needs to change, and that I need to be the one to change it. And I know—I *know*—that if you're patient with me, what I find on the other end of it, once the towers have burned down, will be you."

She looks like she wants to believe me, but then her face clouds again.

"Maybe I just moved too fast for you," she says. "Maybe it was stupid for me to kiss you like that."

"No," I say. "It was amazing. It was the most romantic moment of my life. I've replayed it thousands of times since it happened. I want to kiss you again. Please trust me. I want to kiss you *right now,* but you deserve to be kissed by someone who has her shit together. So I'm going to get my shit together, and then, if you still want me, I'm going to kiss you."

She cocks her head; a smile emerges.

"And until then?" she asks.

"It shouldn't be long. That's what Kylie said, right? And until then, I don't know. Let's just be together. There's a poetry slam tonight. . . ."

"Yeah, everyone's going," she says.

"Will you go with me?"

"Sure," she says.

"Oh, and Mark, too."

She laughs.

"It's a very good thing that Mark is so charming."

She takes my hand.

"Is this okay?" she asks, and she bites her lip, looks at my mouth. She rubs her thumb along my palm. "I need something to tide me over until you're ready for more."

My knees turn weak again. I'm about to lose my resolve.

And then, "Um, *hi*?"

My body tenses. It's Lehna. Of course. June and Uma, both wide-eyed, stand behind her.

I move to step away from Violet, but she keeps her hand in mine.

"Look who I ran into!" she says.

Her voice is so happy.

"Wow," Lehna musters. "What a coincidence."

June's face reddens. She's lucky Lehna's looking at us and not at her.

"You just happened to be here?" she asks me. "By yourself?"

"Mark's here, too."

"I should have known that, I guess."

It weirds me out, the way she says it—all chirpy and pleasant when I know she's neither of those things.

"We're gonna play the button game," Uma says. "A new round starts in three minutes. Want to come?"

"I should find Mark," I say.

"Violet?" Lehna says.

"I'm actually going to hang out with Kate tonight. She's going to the slam, too, so can we reconnect there?"

Shock flashes across Lehna's face, but she transforms it into a smile.

"Oh!" she says. "Wow! Good for you guys!"

And now I realize what's happening. Violet doesn't know that anything is wrong between us. Lehna, for some reason, has been pretending that she and I are fine when really we aren't fine at all. Really we're bad enough that the awfulness of us is creeping in even in this moment, even when Violet is stepping closer to me.

A beep comes from another wing of the museum.

"It's starting soon!" June says. "We have to find some open buttons."

Lehna nods.

"Right," she says. "The button game. Well, have fun, you guys. Text me later."

And then they're heading away from us, back into the crowd.

"Is it just me or was Lehna acting kind of strange?" Violet asks.

"Things between us have been a little . . . tense," I say.

"Why?"

"I don't know. Various reasons. It'll be fine."

"Okay," she says, but she sounds unsure.

"Really," I say. "I'm going to work it out with her, but not right now. Let's go find Mark."

She nods and we hold hands as we make our way back to the shadow room. On our way we pass a group of people at one of the button stands. They're frantically hitting their buttons—some red, some blue—while others around them watch the score on a screen and cheer.

"What *is* the button game?" Violet asks.

"There are people at these stands all over the museum. You try to get your color to win."

"Win at what?"

"Nothing, really. Just the number of pushes."

"What's the point of that?"

"Exactly," I say. "It's like a social phenomenon or something."

I spot Mark outside the shadow room.

"You got sick of it?" I ask him.

"No," he says. "Just letting some other people's shadows have turns in the spotlight."

"That's very thoughtful of you," Violet says, and her smile would be heartbreakingly pretty except that I have little reason to be heartbroken. So instead it's gloriously pretty. Spectacularly pretty. I can't stop looking at her—that's how pretty it is.

"So apparently things went well," Mark says to me.

"I'm working on it," I say, looking at Violet. "I'm trying to make things up to her."

"And is she doing a good job?"

"So far so good," she says.

"I'm glad, because you are clearly the girl for my friend."

"But what about *you*?" Violet says. "First it was 'I'd fight for you,' 'I need you,' and now, as of last night, there's someone new on the horizon."

"She was pretty persuasive, wasn't she?" Mark says. "I mean, I was skeptical, but now I can't get it out of my head. It just feels . . ."

"True," Violet says.

Mark nods.

I say, "We've been on the lookout for all the scenic guys at school."

Violet laughs.

"Scenic. I love that."

"And tonight's this poetry slam. Has Katie invited you yet?"

"Yes, and I have accepted."

"Ryan will be there."

"Uh-oh."

"But other guys, too."

"Scenic guys," Violet says.

"Yes. The vast majority of the guys there will be scenic."

"Excellent."

"But before we go," Mark says, "we need to get a shadow shot of all three of us."

We head into the room and strike poses, waiting for the rest of the people in there to lose interest. One by one, they do, until it's just the three of us. It's dark and the clock is counting down from thirty seconds.

"Let's make a chain," Violet says. "Stretch out our arms and touch fingers."

She walks to one side of me and Mark walks to the other. We hold our arms straight out like wings, our fingers touching at the tips.

"Thirty seconds," Mark says.

This doesn't feel like the card with the burning tower. I've taken a risk, asked Violet to trust me. But I haven't jumped from a burning building or crashed on the rocks. I haven't upended my life.

"Twenty-five!"

What could I do that would be so dramatic? That would change my trajectory, that would set me free?

"Ten!" Mark says.

"Hold steady, everyone!" says Violet.

My heart is so full.

This is what's right. These two beautiful people. Our fingers touching, counting down together.

"Five seconds!" Mark says.

"My arms hurt!" says Violet.

My arms hurt, too, but I would keep them extended like this for so much longer if it meant we could stay here. If I could have them by my side, and graduation wasn't in a few days, and the summer wasn't fleeting.

"Three!" Mark says.

"Two!" Violet yelps.

"One!" we all shout.

A flash of light.

A dropping of our arms.

A stepping forward to see what the wall will hold.

A few seconds pass before our shadows appear, a perfect chain of three. And in those seconds, between darkness and light, I discover what I need to do.

MARK

17

Five nights ago, Katie and I were wandering around a crowded mansion and I felt more lost than I ever had in my life. I felt like a pretender, an intruder, a party crasher, with the party being what the rich and the famous knew as life. It didn't matter that people were calling me beautiful, offering me drinks and propositions that went along with the drinks. It didn't matter that pretending was the point. It didn't matter that Katie was right beside me, just as out of place as I was. I felt everyone was humoring me. I felt they could see how terrified I was, and that as soon as I left the room, they would laugh and shake their heads.

Now we're in a completely different place, and I still can't find my footing. We're in the rec room of a small community center, plastic bottles of cranberry juice and Sprite taking the place of champagne, vodka, and gin. The ceiling and walls are draped with pink and purple streamers, and a dozen tables have been set up in a semicircle around a makeshift stage—basically, a mic stand with an area of space cleared around it.

Ryan is sitting at one of the tables with Taylor and his friends. I don't want to look at Taylor too closely, but I can't look away. He has his footing, and he's dancing all around— keeping one hand on Ryan's arm the whole time. It's strange to see them, especially to see their dynamic together. Ryan is clearly the younger one, clearly the less experienced one, clearly the newbie in this arrangement. Taylor is taking care of him.

I am not used to seeing Ryan like that.

He doesn't spot me at first. I hang back, look instead at Katie and Violet. I have no idea what they said to each other, but the result is visible: They have found each other at last. And with every minute, they are finding each other more.

I told them they didn't have to come with me, that they could abandon their third wheel and he would be fine.

"No way," Katie said. "We're a tricycle, and a tricycle goes nowhere without all three wheels."

Now both of them are studying me, seeing me trying to avoid the fact that Ryan doesn't look up the minute I walk into a room. Like there's any reason he would, when he has Taylor right there.

"Go say hi," Violet prods. "Stake your claim."

But before I can do that, Quinn sashays over. He's wearing a pink tuxedo with a pink carnation in the lapel.

Very subtle, I hear Ryan whisper in my head.

"Be still, my gay, gay heart," Quinn purrs, "but it seems

like the traffic's gotten hella Sapphic. Katiegirl, have you brought the woman of your dreams to our shindig this evening?"

Katie blushes. And once she realizes she's blushing, she blushes even more.

"*Enchanté,*" Violet says, offering her hand. Rather than shake it, Quinn lifts it to his lips.

"*Enchanté!*" he echoes.

I look back over at Ryan, and, yes, he's watching us now. When he sees he's caught my eye, he waves. Taylor notices the gesture, then looks over to me, too. He joins Ryan in waving.

"Go on," Katie says.

It can't be more than fifteen feet, but the time it takes for me to get to them is immeasurably awkward. And it's even more awkward when I get there and Taylor stands up to greet me.

"At last!" he says as he wraps me in a hug. Then, when he pulls out of it, he adds, "I mean, usually I get to meet a guy *before* I see him in his skivvies, but I guess in your case, I'll make an exception."

"I'm so glad you're here," Ryan says, also standing, but not giving me a hug. He introduces me to Taylor's friends, and I miss all of their names. They offer to make space for me at their table, but I indicate the lesbians I came in with and say I should probably sit with them.

"Good man," Taylor says.

I am trying very hard not to hate you, but you're not making it easy, I don't say in response.

Quinn has made his way to the mic and is telling everyone the slam is about to begin.

"Anyone who wants to sign up should do so right away. We only have six poets on the list so far. Listen, people—don't make me go to free swim, because you *know* this lifeguard will drag people *into* the water."

"I dare you to put your name on there," I say to Ryan.

He smirks. "Oh, Belated Barnaby, I already have."

People are taking their seats. I see Lehna skulk in and sit at a table in the back with June and Uma. Violet tries to signal them to come over, but Lehna shakes her head.

I wish Ryan good luck, then walk back.

"How'd that go?" Katie asks when I sit down.

"What am I doing here?" I reply.

I am not a poet. I am a baseball player whose heart is being broken by a poet. There's a difference.

Quinn calls the slam to order. "As you all know, this event is a fund-raiser for The Angel Project, which helps queer youth here in San Francisco, most of them from the streets or from really horrible home conditions. Our first poet, Greer, currently lives in The Angel Project's youth residence. I think it's fitting that we should start with them."

Greer steps to the mic, wearing a red-and-white polka-dot bow tie and a nervous-but-determined expression.

"Thanks, Quinn. As he said, my name is Greer. I was kicked out of my house because my parents couldn't deal with me being genderqueer. This was in California, only about two hours from here. Like so many other people, I decided to come to San Francisco, because it's supposedly the most tolerant place in the world. I quickly found out that tolerance doesn't necessarily translate into a job and a place to live. Things got very desperate, until I found The Angel Project. They gave me support and helped me figure things out. So I'd like to dedicate this one to them."

The audience has grown still, respectful. Katie reaches

for Violet's hand. Then, seeing me notice, she takes my hand, too.

Greer doesn't have any paper in front of them. It's all from memory.

When I was little I loved to paint—
the brush was a plastic wand
with a punk-rock haircut at its tip,
while the colors sat like candies in their tray.
If you wanted orange, you'd introduce red to yellow.
If you wanted green, yellow would have an affair with blue.
Like any kid who isn't encouraged to question,
I had been taught the meaning of colors—
blue and pink, most of all.
We all knew which one princesses wore.
We all knew why I was given so many princesses to paint.

But one day I wondered what would happen
if I mixed the pink and the blue.
One day I reached down to the level of curiosity,
having no idea that it was standing on the shoulders of
    truth.
I thought blue and pink would make the most spectacular
    color—
I took my wand and gathered the blue, laying it on the
    absorbent page
of a coloring book bought to keep me quiet in a Walmart.
Then, without washing the wand clean, I dipped into the
    pink.
This, I was sure, would be the secret to all beauty.

What happened was mud,
dirty sidewalk,
murk.
I had failed.

I pulled away from my curiosity, and the truth underneath.
I trusted other people to teach me the meaning of colors,
and they taught me the wrong things.

It took a long time for the truth to rise up,
and for me to rise up to meet it.
I took out my old paints and I mixed those colors again.
I got the same result, but this time I saw it a different way.
Blue and pink make mud, make dirt, make rock.

I am mud, I am dirt, I am rock.
I am nature, a force of nature.
I am the color that remains when everything else is
    washed away.
I am the color of the ground you walk on, the ground that
    keeps you
from falling. I am elemental, essential,
and that has as much color as any rainbow.

Tell them that. When children ask you, tell them that.

Even though it's a small room, the applause is big. Greer sits back at their table to hugs and high-fives from their friends. Then Quinn gets up and announces that the next poet is going to be . . . Taylor.

Don't react, I tell myself. *Don't check, but assume that Ryan is looking at you.*

Which is silly, because when I do check, Ryan is watching Taylor take the stage.

"That was amazing, Greer," Taylor says when he gets there. "And I can only second what you have to say about The Angel Project. As many of you know, I volunteer there now. But much more important is what they did for me three long, quick years ago. I think it's safe to say that if it weren't for The Angel Project, I wouldn't be here now. I don't mean in this room—I mean on this planet. So it's completely inappropriate for me to say thank you with a poem that has nothing to do with that. I'd tell you its title, but you can probably figure it out."

I look at Ryan and he's not surprised. He knows all this about Taylor already. They've already gone there.

With a jokingly theatrical bow, Taylor reads his poem.

Queen,
understand
everything
exists
reactively.

Please
remember
I
don't
erase

quietly.
Urge,
excite,
embolden,
roar.

Passivity
relinquishes
ideas,
denies
equality.

Quick—
unearth
each
eager
revolution

pulsing
rhythmically
inside.
Desire,
emerge.

There's some applause. I figure Taylor will leave, but instead he says, "Since that was a short one, and since I end it with desire emerging, I'd like to close with a sex poem. With apologies to e. e. cummings—which is, incidentally, my porn name. Here we go, sailors! I wrote this one last night."

> what a trip
> to slip-dip-drip
> nestle
> mortar-pestle
> after
> startle-tickle-
> wrestle
>
> bedhead beauty
> you astonish me
> to a
> dense-sense
> rapture capture
>
> be the holder
> of this beholder
> bolder
> bolder
> we rearrange the universe
> (bolder)
> with our bodies

Taylor finishes with a smile and gets hoots of appreciation in return, as well as more applause. Ryan is applauding with everyone else, but he also looks a little bashful—he wants Taylor to see him applauding, but he doesn't want anyone else to be looking at him or assuming anything from what Taylor's just read. But who does he think he's fooling? When Taylor gets back to the table, he gives Ryan this gigantic confirmation of a kiss, right there in front of everyone else.

"So not necessary," Katie grumbles, and I love her for it.

"Get a room zoom bloom for your skanky hanky-panky!" Quinn shouts out. Taylor actually looks embarrassed now and settles down in his chair, leaving Ryan's mouth alone. His friends lean in to congratulate him. Ryan looks anywhere but at me.

Quinn continues. "The time has come for my own contribution. Some of you may have heard it before—I guess it's what I'm most compelled to share. Each time I come back to it, a few words change. Maybe one day I'll get it to say everything I'm trying to tell. It's called 'The Beat.'"

What happens next is hard to describe. Quinn opens his mouth and it's a different voice that comes out. Raw. Defiant. He's not playing now. He's testifying.

No son of mine, Lord.
No son of mine!
Beat beat beat
You try to beat it out of me
Belt it out of me
Heartless heart
Beat beating
You think you can bruise me
Out of being
Bruise it out of me
When you belt it beat it
Try to break it—
Break the thing you cannot break
Because I carry it so deep inside
No beat of yours no belt of yours
Will ever come close.

You try to beat it out of me
Belt it out of me
Belt me into buckling
Beat me into heartstopping
Stophurting
Trying so hard
You say you'll kill me to save me
Kill the me inside of me
Beat it belt it but it
Just won't budge.
Not for you.

I know
You can't stay in this room forever
I know
We can't stay in this room forever
You beat me belt me to get to me
But you'll never get to me
Not the me me heartbeat me.

I am saving it.

I am saving it for tonight
I am saving it for you right there
And you over there.
I am saving it for
Every you with a me deep inside.
Now that I've left that room
Out into the world as big
As a billion rooms
I have saved me
Yes, I have saved me
Constructed of words and hurt
And the glass self I've protected
All this time
To get to this one of a billion rooms
This room tonight.

Beat beat beat
I have found my own beat
My own pitter-patter
My own sis-boom-bah!
Beat beat beat
I belt it out

Song sung strong
Stung song
Tongue song
Back from being
Bitten back
Some songs sung
Beg to be carried home.
This song sings
To be carried far and wide.
Beat beat beat—

The sound it brings
Is the sound of wings.

When he's done, there is the briefest of silences. Then: noise.
Hands beating together. Voices meeting together. Someone
gets to their feet. We all get to our feet. Katie is crying next to
me. Quinn in front of us is not crying. He is not smiling,
either. He is taking a deep breath, letting it out.

I don't even know how to ask the question I want to ask. "Where did that come from?" is what I say to Katie, and it sounds stupid, inadequate.

"It was awful," Katie tells me. "Freshman year. He had to go to his mom and tell her she either had to kick his father out or he would leave himself. His mother chose Quinn. But it was really touch-and-go."

"I had no idea," I say.

"He wanted school to be normal. It was the only normal he had."

I look over to Ryan—did he know? But I can tell from his expression that he didn't, either. He catches my eye, and we don't need to say a word to have the whole conversation. About how oblivious we were. About how there was so much more to Quinn than we ever gave him credit for.

"Okay, people, *enough*," Quinn says now. "You're only making it harder for our next poet—Ryan Ignatius."

Ryan looks like he wants to pass. Or pass out. Or both. But his whole table is cheering, and Taylor is giving him an encouraging squeeze. *There's no going back now,* I can imagine him thinking. As he picks up some pages from his table and heads to the mic, my secondhand nervousness is about as strong as a firsthand dose. I cheer loudly for him, hoping he can hear my voice, and that it will help.

"Hi," he says when he gets to the mic. "I'm Ryan, and this is my first time."

"You're doing great!" someone from Greer's table shouts.

Ryan's hands are shaking as he unfolds his poem. And they remain shaking as he starts to read. I can't tell whether the first line he reads is the title or the real first line.

I'm not ready.
I'm not ready
to walk three steps ahead of where I am.

I'm not ready
to be paired,
                  declared,
                                  bared
        to be certain
        of what lies behind the curtain.

I'm not ready
to call it by its name
because then it won't be the same
as everything I used to be.

You're so ready
for me to be ready.
But I'm not ready
to put on the clothes you've sewn me.

They're beautiful.
I'm not really sure they'll fit.

You hold me steady,
but I'm not ready.
Not ready to tell you why.
Not ready to be more scared
than I am right now."

He is not looking up. He is looking at the paper. And when the time comes to turn the page, his hands are still shaking so much that he drops it. It slides behind him, lost.

Instead of stopping to pick it up in front of everyone else, he tries to continue from memory.

I'm ready to lose myself,
But—
I mean, I'm ready—
I'm not ready.

Now he looks at the audience. Not at me. Not at Taylor. At someone else. Anybody else.

> I'm not ready
> to do this,
> to stand here

I think this is part of the poem. But maybe it isn't part of the poem. Because Ryan stops. Freezes. Says, "I'm sorry," puts down the mic, and walks—not runs, walks—out of the room.

Violet starts clapping. Other people join in. And I am a minute too late. I am frozen, too. Before I can get up, Taylor is up. Before I can follow Ryan, Taylor is following Ryan. Taylor is closer to the door. I freeze again. I look at Katie, but Katie's not going to tell me to go. It's Violet who tells me to go. Tells me to hurry.

So I stand up, even though Quinn is announcing the next poet, who is not me. People think it's me, though, because of the timing of my standing up, and they're even more confused when I head in the opposite direction from the stage, when I head out the door.

Ryan and Taylor haven't gotten far. They're right outside. Taylor has Ryan in his arms, is telling him he was amazing, that he was brave, that the first step is always, always the hardest. All the right things to say, only they're in his voice, not mine. I stop heading toward them, but they've already heard me. They pull apart a little, look at me.

I am interrupting.

For some reason, it's Taylor I find myself talking to. "I just wanted to see if he was okay," I explain.

Taylor nods. Gets it.

"I'm fine," Ryan says. "Really. I guess I'm not that much of an improviser."

Neither, it seems, am I. I just stand there.

"We'll be back in soon," Taylor says.

"Oh yeah. Of course. See ya."

I open the door and it makes what feels like a huge clatter, right in the middle of a really quiet poem. I don't want to draw more attention to myself, so I stand there until the poet is finished—a good ten minutes later.

I make my way back to my table, expecting that Taylor and Ryan will follow on my heels. Taylor said they'd be back soon, after all. But they don't come back. I see the friends at Taylor's table checking texts and whispering to one another. News I don't know.

I check my phone. Nothing.

Someone from Greer's table takes the stage and recites a very funny poem called "Ode to Pee-wee Herman." When it's done, Quinn gets back on to say that since we've now gone through the list, we're going to take a five-minute break—and in that five-minute break he wants to see at least three more people volunteer to spit out some words.

"Do you want to go?" Violet asks us.

I want to go, but I'm not sure I want to say I want to go.

Katie settles it by observing, "If we leave now, Quinn will kill us," which is probably true.

So we sit there. Some of Taylor's friends are up and talking to the people at the table next to ours, so I can't tell Katie what happened in the hallway. I can sense she's correctly assuming it wasn't good.

Quinn comes over, and it's while Violet and Katie are telling him how amazing his poem was that I look over to the stage area and see the lone piece of paper resting at the base of the back wall. The second page of Ryan's poem. It seems wrong to leave it there, so I head over to get it. It's facedown. I guess I could just fold it like that and never discover how the poem ended.

It's not his diary, though. It's something he was planning to read to everyone. So I figure it's okay to look.

Only, after I'm done, it doesn't feel okay.

> I'm ready to lose myself,
> but I'm not ready to lose you.
> I'm ready to find myself,
> But I'm not ready for you to know what I find.
>
> If you want me to change,
> be ready for me to change.
> I don't think you're ready for that.
> I don't think I'm ready for that.
>
> Why do you have to risk the good things
> for the better things?
>
> I'm not ready for the answer.

I know he's gone—they're gone—but I go out into the hall anyway. When I find he's not there, I take out my phone again. But what can I say? That I'm ready for him to change? That I'm ready for him to do what he wants to do? The past few days have shown that's not true.

I guess I'm not ready, either.

Quinn's heading to the mic when I walk in. I put the second page of Ryan's poem on the table. Katie's eyes grow wider as she reads it. And they grow even wider when Quinn surprises us all by announcing, "Welcome back, bitches. The Queer Youth Poetry Slam is now spiked as punch to welcome *Lehna* to the mic!"

THURSDAY

Kate

18

It's a normal Thursday morning in my kitchen. The coffeepot hisses and puffs as it always does; we sit at the round breakfast table as we always do. Mom, as always, reads the business section while Dad, as always, reads about the foreign news first and then cheers himself up with Arts and Entertainment.

We eat toast and fruit and yogurt.

We reach over one another for the box of half-and-half or the jar of honey.

Periodically, we check the bright red clock until one of us says, "Seven thirty," at which point we'll collect and rinse the dishes, put the perishables back in the refrigerator, and walk to our three cars, parked side by side in our wide suburban driveway. I can't even explain the comfort I take in this routine. The comfort could fill the sky—it's that immense.

But I haven't been able to enjoy it for months, because of this thing I've been carrying. This anxiety. This crushing, terrible dread. This weight I decided to shed yesterday in the shadow room, holding hands with Mark and Violet. We were like a paper chain of children. We were substance and shadow. We were heat and clutched hands, and wonder, and love. And that clarity I got—it was breathtaking, it took me by surprise, and then it let me go.

So maybe a normal Thursday morning at the breakfast table is not the right time to do this, but I'm doing it anyway.

"Mom?" I say. "Dad? Can I talk to you guys for a second?"

They lower their sections of the paper.

"Of course," Dad says.

"You can have more than a second," Mom adds, smiling even though I can see her nervousness.

"I've been having a hard time lately."

"Something's happened with Lehna, hasn't it?" Dad says. "The house hasn't been this quiet since you two met."

"Shh," Mom says. "Let her tell us, sweetheart."

"Right. Go on, Katie."

"Yeah," I say. "Lehna and I are going through some stuff. That's part of it, maybe, I don't know. But what I'm really struggling with is college."

Mom cocks her head. Dad takes his glasses off—very, *very* slowly—and presses on the spot between his eyebrows.

"I don't want to go," I say. "Not yet."

"Hmmmm," Mom says.

Dad keeps pressing between his brows. Harder and harder.

"Can you . . . elaborate?" Mom asks.

"Yeah," I say. "Sorry. I just want to defer for a year. Every time I think about leaving I panic. I know it's normal to be nervous, that it's huge—to leave home, fend for myself—so it's expected to feel kind of shaky about it. But I should be a *little* bit excited, too, right? And I'm not. I'm not at all. I can't even think about it because I hate the idea so much."

"You hate the idea," Mom says.

"I do. I hate it. Dad, you're stressing me out. You're going to bruise your face."

"I don't even," Dad says. "I don't even know . . ."

"I think what your father is saying is that we need a little time to sit with this."

I have no idea what's going on inside her head. Her voice is calm; she's even smiling. But she works in the Human Resources department at an investment firm. She's used to telling people what they've done wrong in a way that makes them feel good about themselves. She's used to firing people and making it sound like an opportunity.

"Fair," I say. "It's seven thirty anyway."

We all rise. Dad puts his glasses back on.

"We love you, Katie," Dad says.

"Kate," Mom corrects.

"Right," he says. "Kate. We'll pick this up later on, okay? When we have more time."

I nod. We clear the dishes and we rinse them. We grab our bags and hoist them over our shoulders. We walk single file out the door and to our three cars.

"Just a year," I say, before we all slide in.

My mother nods. My father sighs.

And then they pull away, and I hear my phone ringing from the back. I haven't left yet, so I jump out and get my bag, and I look at the caller.

Ryan. His name on my screen takes me by surprise. We

haven't texted since last year when we were working on the lit mag cover. I had forgotten that I even had his number.

"You answered," he says. "Are you with him?"

"Mark?" I say. "No. I'm on my way to pick him up."

"What's he doing?"

"Um . . . getting ready for school I'd imagine?"

"Not right this second. That's not what I meant. Or maybe I did. Right now he's probably finishing his homework for first period. Or brushing his teeth? He brushes his teeth a lot. Like *a lot* a lot. Or maybe that's just because he thought we might be making out and he was trying to be prepared. I never thought about that, but it's probably what it was."

"Hey," I say. "Are you okay?"

"No. I don't know. I'm tired. I didn't sleep."

"At all?"

"He saw the poem, right? I mean the rest of it, right? I know he did. I can just feel it. And his phone was off. Off at midnight, off at two, off at five, off at seven. It's just been totally . . . *off*."

"Yeah," I say. "He read the rest of it."

"He did?"

"Yeah."

"I knew it. We left. I was . . . upset. At least that's what Taylor kept saying, 'You're upset. You're upset,' and he said we should probably leave, so we left. And then we got back to his place and I remembered that I dropped my poem. That it was just lying there on the stage somewhere, all alone, for anyone to find and make fun of, and I panicked. I left him and I ran all the way back, and everything was over and almost everyone was gone, but they let me back in anyway and I looked all over the stage, but it wasn't there. But then I found it, and it was face up, right there on the table, and I *knew* it. I knew he'd read it. How did he react?"

"You should probably ask him that yourself," I say.

"I told you already! His phone. Is fucking. *Off*."

"Then ask him at school."

"I don't think I can go to school today. I'm not really feeling well."

I want to tell him he doesn't need to state the obvious. I didn't know Ryan was capable of this kind of emotion. I thought he was all literary allusion and little feeling, all critic and no poet. But then I think of him onstage last night, all tremor and fear, and I feel myself softening for him, even though he's crushed my friend's heart and might not deserve my sympathy.

"Are you okay, Ryan?" I ask him. "That's a sincere question and I want a sincere answer."

Silence.

"Ryan?"

"I don't think so."

"Okay," I say. "Just breathe. We'll be there soon."

Mark's waiting for me when I pull up to his house. He looks a little worn-out himself, and I can't help it—I reach out and mess up his floppy, all-American boy hair.

"Is that really necessary?" he asks, but I can tell that he didn't really mind.

"Where does Ryan live?"

"Why?"

"Because that's where we're headed."

"You know," Mark says, "there's this thing called 'first period'? And then this other thing called 'first period on the second to last school day of the year'?"

"Address," I say.

"Howard Street. Behind the Seven-Eleven."

"Thank you."

"What's this about?" he asks as I drive.

"You'd know if you turned on your phone."

"Maybe I kept my phone off precisely so that I wouldn't *have* to know."

"Then you should be happy that he called me so that I could tell you this: Your friend needs you. It might not be fair. It might really suck, because you've needed him and he's been off *slip-dip-dripping* with a college boy—"

"Don't forget *mortar-pestling*."

"Oh, I haven't. Nor have I forgotten rearranging the universe—"

"—with their *bodies*—"

"—which last time I checked is a pretty big accomplishment. I mean, not just anyone can do that."

"Apparently not me," he says. "Or else Ryan wouldn't have had to trade me in for his erotic poet."

"Nope," I say. "No time for self-pity this morning. You have some rescuing to do. Which house?"

"The blue one."

I pull over. I turn off the Jeep and turn to Mark.

"He sounds like shit," I say. "It sounds serious. I'm gonna be right here. Let me know if you need me."

Mark takes a breath. Shakes his head. I can tell he really doesn't want to do this, but he gets out of the Jeep anyway. I expect him to knock, but he turns the knob and lets himself into the house, and yeah, that makes sense. Because up until a few days ago, nothing was wrong between them—not on the surface, anyway. A few days ago, Mark was a quiet kid in my math class, a blur of motion in the outfield at the one baseball game I ever attended. So much can change in a few days, even in a few hours. I've brought him here to face the change head-on and I know I'm going to have to face it, too.

I'm not running away from anything anymore.

It's a promise I'm making to myself.

You can keep doing what you're supposed to, what you're expected to, and tell yourself it's what you want. Sit with the same people at lunch, pretending you still have things in common. Read the shiny college brochures, go on the tours, buy into the myth that one of them is meant for you. Believe, at eighteen, that you know what your life will hold and how to prepare for it.

But if you don't really believe it, if all that time you're harboring a doubt so deep it creeps into even your best moments, and you break the rules and step away, then there's going to be a reckoning. You are going to have to explain yourself.

As I sit in the driveway and wait, last night rushes back, takes me over. I'm sitting in that uncomfortable chair, already wrecked by Quinn's poem, by Ryan's exit, by Mark's defeat. And now here's Lehna.

"I don't usually write poetry," she says. "But I had this in my journal from the other night and I figured, I don't know, why not."

She blinks against the lights into the audience. "Go, Lehna!" Violet shouts. June and Uma wave with great enthusiasm. But I just watch her, bracing myself for what might come.

"Okay," she says. "Here it goes."

> We were swimming downstream, always.
> We were all scales and fins,
> all gleaming in the sun,
> all carefree and careless.
> We never had to try hard

or even try at all.
You and me,
me and you,
and the water,
and the sun.

Or, no.

What we really were,
were twins.
The kind that feel it
when the other is cold.
The kind that always hears
two heartbeats
instead of one.
Pinch me
and you'd say
ouch.

Or maybe
I imagined all of it:
the water,
the sun,
even our scales and fins.
Maybe it was just circumstance
and nothing profound
or anomalous
or even
unusual,
the way you'd eat a strawberry
and I'd say
yum.
Because all it took
was for you to step away
for me to hear
a single heartbeat.

It was always
just me.
It was always
just you.
We thought we were special,
but we were always
the subjects
of two separate
sentences.

"Okay," she said. "That's it."

And I know things happened after that. The rise of applause, everyone's teary eyes. Mark leaning over to me, saying, "Wow. So she *is* human." Violet's questioning look and whatever it is I must have told her. But everything that happened after, it was a blur, because all I remember is Lehna, blinking into the bright light, and the way it sank into me, burrowing, festering: Whatever this is that's happening between us, it's another part of the tower that I have to burn down.

MARK

19

I dare you.

Why do we think this is okay? Why do we always feel the need to push and push and push? Don't we know that pushing is never a way to get a person to come closer?

And yet.

There is something powerful about the shedding of comfort. There is something intense about feeling that person push, knowing that the force behind it is the force of their caring, of their genuine belief that the push will get you to a better place.

I'm not ready.

As I'm walking up the stairs to Ryan's room, I'm thinking the only real response to this statement could be:

Who is?

* * *

He's still in his pajamas. Which isn't fair, because in Ryan's case pajamas means boxers and a ratty old Queen Amidala T-shirt that is much sexier than any late-nineties relic should ever be.

But that's not what's being drawn into my focus. What I'm seeing is a boy so lost in the world that he can't get himself out of bed. The tiredness from lack of sleep, the tiredness of too many thoughts without hitting on the right one. He looks like a balloon that once touched the ceiling brightly but now, weeks later, stumbles along the floor.

"Thanks for coming," he says. And the fact that he feels the need to thank me makes me sad. It should be understood that I would be here, that I will always be here.

"I know it's ridiculous," he goes on. "The timing, I mean. For fuck's sake, there are only *two days left* in school. You would have thought I could've stayed in the closet for two more days. But no. That, apparently, was not the plan."

"So this is it?" I ask. "Today's the day?"

He pats a space next to him on the bed, then clutches a pillow to his chest. I sit down where he's gestured me to sit, facing him.

"Today has been the day for a very long time," he tells me. "Today has been something I've told myself often without ever really believing it. But this week—today actually became *today*. No more looking at a wall and pretending it was a mirror. No more shelving the fiction in the nonfiction section. No more thinking I could get away with it. I know you don't want to hear it, but it was Taylor who called my bluff. With you and me, the secrecy was part of the story—at least the way I was writing it. I know you would have written it differently. But with me and him—I had to leave the world I'd created. I had to walk into the world that really was. The feelings I'm feeling—they are not tomorrow feelings. They're today feelings. With you and me—it's just so . . ."

"Complicated?" I volunteer.

"Yeah. Complicated. Can I tell you another thing you don't want to hear?"

"Sure."

"If I hadn't seen you up there on that bar—I never would have had the courage to talk to Taylor. To dance with him. To let all this happen. You gave me the inspiration I needed. Part of it was competition, I'm sure—you did that thing so I had to do something even riskier. But part of it was sheer admiration. So I flirted with him so openly—and doing that made me realize what open felt like. I got to that point. I'm at that point. Now I just have to figure out the other ninety-nine percent of it. And you know what? That other ninety-nine percent is *fucking scary*."

I nod. It is.

I see how truly terrified he is. In a twisted way, I am glad that I am part of it. And in an equally twisted way, I am sad that I am only a part of it and not all of it.

But that is not what this is about.

I know that is not what this is about.

My heart goes out to him, but in a different way from before. It used to want affection. Attention. Recognition.

Now it just wants for him to find his way. And it knows that his way and mine might not be the same.

I know him well. There was a blind spot in my knowing. But now I'm looking around it. I am knowing him more truthfully.

"I'm sorry," he says, and what he's apologizing for is the fact that he's upset, that I am seeing him upset. He knows me well, too.

"There's no need to be," I assure him.

Now he says something else—another kind of apology. "I really like him."

"That's okay. Really, it is."

I look at him in his Star Wars T-shirt and anchor-print boxers, clutching a pillow on this bed we have spent so much of our time in, and what I realize is that somehow, without even knowing it, I have stepped out of love with him, and where I've stepped instead may end up being the better place. I *have to* step out of love with him, because the ground I've always wanted to be there was never really there. He is capable of giving that ground, but I am not the one he wants to give it to. Instead I have the ground we've grown all these years. I love him indestructibly, and I care about him at a root level, but in this three-breath-long moment I can understand that the two of us will never be boyfriends, never be husbands, never be everything to each other in that way. I can let that go, and hold tight to everything else.

It should feel like a retreat. It should feel like my love is diminishing and my feelings are contracting. But instead I have a sense that they're expanding. And they are doing it because they have to.

I am sure that later on I will doubt this. I know that I will regret it, that I will wonder if this sudden understanding was just a trick of the light. But there are no illusions here. Today is finally today. We are no longer what we were. We are now what we're going to be.

"I know you're not ready," I tell him. "I'm not ready, either.

But you know what? It's happening anyway. And we're going to be okay. We'll risk the good thing for the better thing. We're really, truly going to be okay."

I feel nearly empty as I finish this sentence. I've pulled out as much of myself as I can, and I am offering it to him now, no longer a part of me but not entirely relinquished. And in return, he lets go of the pillow. He opens his arms and says my name over and over, as if at long last he's found me, as if at long last we understand that this is what we needed to learn.

Katie is still waiting for me outside.

Of course she is.

I get into the passenger seat, but I don't close the door. I don't want her to drive away.

"How'd it go?" she asks.

"I don't think either Ryan or I will be going to school today."

"Oh wow. Meaning . . . ?"

"Meaning that although for some reason National Coming Out Day is not, in fact, a part of Pride Week, we are rearranging the calendar so Ryan can have his own Coming Out Day. Movies like *Pride* and old episodes of *Glee* will be watched. Ice cream will be eaten. There may be some wild dancing to Robyn and Rihanna. You never know."

"Ice cream? Is that really part of the coming-out process?"

"Hells yes. Ben and Jerry have lasted so long together—they're our role models."

"And then . . . ?"

"And then we might invite Taylor over. So I can get to know him, since it looks like he's my best friend's boyfriend."

I try to say this casually, but I stumble a little. After all, it's the first time I've ever had to say it.

"Oh, Mark," Katie says, concerned. "Is that really smart? You don't have to do that."

"No, it's okay. I'm told that if you're going to fall in love with someone, it's always best to fall for someone who's going to love you back. That's never going to happen with Ryan, and I am strangely okay with it. At least for now."

"The heart is a treacherous beast."

"But it means well."

Katie smiles. "Yes—*the heart is a treacherous beast, but it means well.* That just about sums it up."

"What they never tell you is that it's actually the friend-ship part that's harder. Kissing is easy. Kissing has its own politics, but at the end of the day, it's kissing. It's the real stuff—the being-part-of-each-other's-lives piece of it—"

"—being close to twins without being twins—"

"Yes! That is both the challenge and the reward."

I look at Katie and know that sometimes it isn't all that hard, that sometimes you can just fall into step with some-one and keep pace for a good long time. Again, it amazes me that a week ago we barely knew each other's names. Now we're on this journey together. I know I can only help her so much and she can only help me so much—ultimately, we have to solve our own problems. But it helps to have someone else in step. It helps to have someone to talk to when it's time to take a break from solving everything.

"So," I say, "do you think you'll be talking to Lehna today?" It was obvious last night from her shell-shocked reac-tion to Lehna's poem that Katie needs to resolve some of the sentences they've left dangling.

"I will," she says. And then she says it again, as if the first time wasn't certain enough. "I've already talked to my parents about taking a break from the whole college plot. And I still need to talk to Violet about where the hell we go from here. I've loved her wandering heart for so long . . . but I have no idea what all that wandering means for her and me. I feel the urge for going, but I have no idea if it's meant to be a solo exploration or not."

"You'll figure it out," I say. Not because it's this vacuous space-filler of a thing to say, but because I genuinely believe it. Katie is going to figure it out. She has enough of the world in her hands to do that.

"Thank you," she says. Then she leans over and gives me a kiss on the cheek. "Now go help that boy find his way. And remember—as supportive as you want to be, if he and Taylor start being all boyfriendly, you have every right to leave the room and get some space. Empathy is wonderful, but you can still overdose on it if you try too much too fast. Noted?"

"Noted."

"And while I will turn a blind eye to your willful disregard of your educational responsibilities today, I shall fully expect to be seeing you tomorrow for the grand finale, and again for the full host of Pride Weekend activities, not the least of which is the parade on Sunday. For all her worldliness, Violet's never seen a pride parade, and I swear by Tegan, Sara, *and* the Holy Ghost that we'll be showing her the best one ever."

"It will be Ryan's first as well."

"How lucky they are to have us!" Katie says.

I kiss her back on the cheek and say, "How lucky indeed."

Kate

20

Making my way toward Lehna at lunch, I feel the closest I've ever felt to being one of those lonely freshmen in the first days of school. The unfortunate boys and girls whose families have uprooted them just in time for high school, or the quirky, formerly homeschooled kids, or the kids who live in nearby, more dangerous towns and have found their way, through lottery luck or parental cunning, to our suburban haven of a school.

Lehna and I use to say blessings for them. *Let purple backpack kid with the scarf find his people. Pigtailed girl with brand-new white Converse, head north to the circle of girls with their Sharpies out and make those shoes your own.*

Eventually, unless they were very unlucky, each of them

would find somewhere to belong, but for those first self-conscious, wandering days when they nibbled their sandwiches with their heads down, Lehna and I agonized on their behalf. We had arrived at school hand in hand, both of us newly out to the world with a summer's worth of scavenged rainbow paraphernalia gracing our backpacks. Rainbow friendship bracelets, *Legalize Gay* T-shirts, the paper bag covers for our textbooks emblazoned with all the Tegan and Sara songs we knew by heart, which was every one of them.

We were beacons to the other queer kids. We got the hard part over with in eighth grade. No awkward boys asking us to Homecoming, *thankyouverymuch*. June and Uma, then strangers to us and each other, found us by the rainbow glow of our backpacks. A boy named Hank found us, too, and for six months he filled our lives with comic books and Frank Ocean. And then he started dating Quinn and his parents found out, and he began his slow fade from our school and, eventually, from our lives altogether.

We should have known it already—the world was trying to tell us in so many ways—but Hank is the one who taught us that life wasn't so easy for all of us. Hank is the one who told Lehna and me that we were lucky. Hank is the one who made luck a sometimes complicated thing.

And it's Hank I'm thinking about now, as I step down to where my friends are lounging, their backs to me, on the senior deck. They're looking out at the rest of the school from this hard-won place of seniority. I set my backpack down next to Lehna. I get out my phone and pull up Frank Ocean's "Super Rich Kids." I turn the volume up as loud as it'll go and set it on the railing in front of us.

We bob our heads and listen.

When it's over, Uma says, "He should be here with us."

June says, "I went on a rampage once, trying to find him online. I searched everywhere. I even thought of all the fake names he might use."

"I did that once, too," Uma says.

"Kate and I did, too," Lehna says. "And I thought I saw him once, on Telegraph. I called his name, but he didn't look up."

"We were so young when we were friends." It's the kind of proclamation adults would roll their eyes over, but it's true. "We were *fourteen*. His voice hadn't even changed. He was skinny like a little kid. I don't know if I'd even recognize him now."

"Hank," June says. "We are sending you our love, wherever you are."

We sit in silence for a little while, and then I say, "I have something to tell you guys."

"Let me guess. You and Mark are getting married."

"Come on, Lehna," June says, and we all turn to her, surprised. "*What?* Things feel normal for the first time in a week. Let's just try to stay positive, okay?"

"Well, *okay*," Lehna says. "Sorry, everyone. Kate, go ahead."

"I'm going to take a gap year."

"Seriously?" Uma says. "What are you going to do?"

"I don't know yet."

"But where did this come from?" June asks. "You never even mentioned it. Like, not even as an idea."

"I know," I say. "It just kind of came to me."

"But aren't you excited about college?" Uma asks.

"Only in a distant-future kind of way." I feel Lehna looking at me, not critically, but like she's really listening. I see my opening. I take it: "Distant, like the way I think of my wedding day with Mark."

"Right," Lehna says. "You in your white veil, him in his black tux."

"I know it will happen, but I have to sow my oats first."

"Work your way through the rest of the baseball players."

"Only the Varsity team."

"All those muscles. Those skintight pants, that sexy *bulge*—"

"Excuse me, but this is actually pretty serious," June says.

"Is it?" I ask. "I don't know."

"Um, *yeah*. We're talking about your future. We all worked hard to get into our colleges."

"And I'm still going to go to college. It's just . . ." I wrack my brain for a good reason to give them, and then I give up and just say what's true. "I want to let things be messy. I want to be free, but only as free as feels right in the moment. And," I say, "I want to be with Violet."

"Oh," June breathes.

"Oh," Uma echoes.

"Love," they say.

"Maybe," I say, because it's more prudent than yes, because it's been less than a week since our first kiss, fewer than twenty-four hours since I asked her to trust me. I say maybe because when you're a teenager there's this rule: You aren't supposed to make decisions based on love. You are supposed to tell your heart that it's an immature and fickle thing. You're supposed to remind yourself of Romeo and Juliet and how badly it turned out for them.

Your poor teenage heart. It isn't equipped for decisions like this.

Except maybe. *Maybe*. It is.

I still need to talk to Lehna.

Lunch ends and we head to our lockers together.

"What are you doing after school?" I ask her.

"Going over to Shelbie's. Candace is going to be there, so we're all going to grab some dinner."

"Want to get coffee first? I'm heading over there, too."

"To see Violet?"

"Yeah, and I have to stop by AntlerThorn. I got a message from Brad. Something about the auction."

"Oh yeah. Congrats on that, by the way."

"On what?"

"Your painting."

"What about it?"

"The bidding had just ended when we left the show that night. Yours sold for a lot."

"Really?"

She laughs, amazed that I don't know this already.

"Yeah. Like, thousands. I was too pissed for it to totally register, but I know it raised more money than any of the others. Anyway," she says. "Yeah. I can do coffee."

It's four hours later, and we're across from each other at a café table in the Mission, identical foam ferns gracing the tops of our cappuccinos. I see the way they match and I just say it.

"Twins."

She shrugs.

"It was a great poem. Everyone thought so," I say.

I think about it now, all the ways we had been twin-like,

with our identical taste in books and music, our simultaneous realizations that we liked girls, the way we never even entertained the thought of us fooling around because sisters just don't do that. We even came out together, gathering both pairs of parents in Lehna's living room as though we were all one family.

"We're lesbians," we said in unison, our sweaty, fourteen-year-old hands clasped.

"Are you a couple?" my dad asked.

We turned to each other, surprise at the suggestion momentarily wiping out our nervousness, and cracked up laughing.

I'm crying now. I didn't see it coming, but here are tears down my cheeks, and then Lehna is crying, too. This café is full of the young and queer and beautiful. Everyone's slightly older than we are; everyone has lived through something like this already. But still. I know that I've ruined something between us. I know that I stopped feeling like Lehna's twin a long time ago, and it's a terrible thing to be the one who walks away.

But it's Lehna who says, "Look. I need to apologize."

"What for?"

"All that bullshit with Violet. Like telling you to reapply your lipstick, and saying you looked normal, and making you come up with a fake gallery show as if who you are isn't good enough."

"Why did you do it?"

"I don't know," she says. "I've been trying to figure it out. It's just this feeling I got ... like you didn't have fun with me anymore. Like I suddenly wasn't interesting enough. And I didn't like feeling that way."

"I don't really know what happened to me," I say.

"You just changed. You went from Katie to Kate. And I don't really think you wanted to take anyone with you." She shakes her head. "It sucks to be left behind."

"I felt so lost," I say.

"And then, what? Mark helped you find yourself?"

"I'm allowed to make other friends."

"Of course you are. And you're *allowed* to switch them out for me like I was just a stand-in for the real thing the whole time. You're *allowed* to replace me, but I'm allowed to be angry about it."

"I wasn't trying to replace you," I say, but even as I get the words out I'm wondering if it's true.

But *now*—as Lehna wipes tears off her face—in *this* moment it's what's true. The thought of losing her forever is impossible.

"It's fine if you make new friends," she says. "We're both going to make new friends. For the first time in our lives we aren't going to live near each other. We aren't even going to live in the same state. I just don't understand why it had to happen now. This is the last week of high school, Kate. These are our last days together. They aren't supposed to be like this."

I nod.

"I know," I say. "I'm sorry."

We stare into our cups. Lehna takes a sip, and I do, too.

"People probably think we're breaking up or something," Lehna says.

I smile, wipe the tears off my face, and look around, but I don't catch anyone paying attention.

"Seems like things are good with Violet," she says.

Even in the midst of all of this, happiness surges up from some deep place within me.

"Yeah," I say.

"I'm glad. You guys are gonna be great together."

"And with Candace?"

She breaks into a slow grin. I recognize her feeling.

Brad waves to me as I step inside the gallery.

"Hey," he says.

I brace myself for his verbal onslaught, but nothing follows.

"*Hey*?" I say. "That's all?"

"Long day. Audra left early. Sometimes a boy's gotta take a break."

"A break from what?"

"From what everyone expects of me," he says. "Come on back."

He leads me through the gallery and up a short flight of stairs, his gait less buoyant than usual. Even his hair is more subdued.

"Welcome to my office," he says.

It's a small space with concrete walls, metal file cabinets, and a fluorescent light.

"Cozy."

"It's a fucking *cell*. I think it's Audra's idea of a joke."

"She's a real sweetheart."

He snorts.

"I just need you to sign this, saying you're giving the proceeds of your painting to the Angel Project."

He hands me a contract.

"Sure," I say.

"We raised over twenty grand for them."

"That's amazing."

"Your painting accounted for almost a third of that."

"Wait, what?"

"Yeah," he says. "Total bidding war."

My hand trembles as I sign my name. I thought Violet was going to be my only collector.

"Garrison's picking it up today. I told him you would be dropping in around now. Mind waiting a few minutes?"

"*Garrison* bought it? I can wait."

We head back into the sunny gallery, and only then do I see my painting. It's hanging on a wall in a prime spot. I see my others, too. I want to throw a sheet over them to spare me my embarrassment. But this one is different. I can see that.

Brad stands beside me and looks.

"I'm going to miss this piece," he says.

I turn to him. His face is pure sincerity.

"That's the best compliment you've given me."

"Is it?"

"Brad. You called my paintings quaint."

"Not this one," he says.

The door swings open, and in rushes the city noise, and then a tall, handsome man.

"Well, look," I say. "It's the manufacturer of my fifteen minutes of fame."

"That fame is not going to be so fleeting," Garrison says. "I swung by the night of the show just to say hello. I didn't find you here, but I did find this painting. I couldn't stop looking at it."

"Thank you," I say. It comes out a whisper—I mean it so much.

"What for?" Brad asks. "He's getting a painting he wants and you're not getting a dime from the sale."

But it isn't about the money. It's about what I know is true. Because I'm looking at this bright red storm of color on a canvas, at all my delicate lines and passionate brushstrokes. I'm looking at something so urgent and true, so far beyond what I thought I was capable of making.

I'm looking at what happens when I let go and trust myself, and the vision of it thrills me.

The cashier at the de Young ticket booth tells me she can't sell me a ticket this near to closing.

"You only have fifteen minutes," she says.

"That's okay," I tell her. "It's worth it."

This is where Violet told me she'd be. She offered to meet me outside when she was finished, but I can't wait another fifteen minutes. I need to see her now.

"There's the observation tower," the woman says. "It's free and open to the public. You still have time to go there. But there's no food allowed."

"Oh, this?" I say, holding up the artichoke I bought on my way over. "It isn't actually food. At least, not in this context. It's a flower."

"Put the flower in your backpack, please."

I text Violet to meet me in the tower and find my way to the elevator.

She's looking out over North Beach when I find her. So many people are up here, taking in the panorama of the city through the glass walls, but there are things I need to say that can't wait. So much is clear to me now.

I touch her shoulder. She turns to face me.

"Hey there," she says.

"The Exploratorium yesterday. The de Young today. Is this a museum tour?"

"It's just a habit, I guess. It's always easy to find the museums, and that way you're guaranteed something good to look at."

I smile.

"But somehow I don't think you're here to discuss my habits," she says. "You look nervous. What's wrong?"

A chime sounds, and then a recorded voice tells us that the museum will be closing in ten minutes. So I rush in and say, "I think I never really wanted to meet you. That's why I ran away from Shelbie's party."

Hurt flashes across her face, but I keep going.

"The idea of you kept saving me, over and over. Every time I felt worried, all I had to do was think of your name and I would be calm again. All of my paintings were about you, but they were also about the idea of another world, another life, one that might feel better than the one I'd been inhabiting. You were my escape. I needed you to keep being an idea to me."

She shrugs, which is not what I'm after. I have to push through this part, though, to get to what I really want to say.

"All those stories Lehna told me about you. I survived on them. I was destined to be disappointed and then what would save me?"

She looks away, but I take her hand.

"Wait," I say. "This time *I'm* not finished. Then something happened: I met you. It didn't matter how much I managed to mess things up in order to prolong the dream of you—you showed up anyway. And you were—you *are*—better than the dream. And I'm realizing now that your job isn't to save me, and I'm okay with that. All I need for you is to be in my life, and I'll figure out the rest of it."

"Be in your life?" she says. "I don't know what you mean by that."

"More than be in my life," I say. "*Much* more than be in my life. I mean I want to be your girlfriend. I want to see you every day. I want to wake up to texts from you that say good morning and I want to kiss you whenever I want to. I want to kiss you right now."

She laughs.

"You really know how to worry a girl," she says. "I mean, a little warning next time would be good. Something like, 'I'm going to say a bunch of things that sound like rejection, but in the end I'll turn it all around and say something good.'"

"I was just being honest!" I say. "The opposite of elusive!"

"Right," she says. "Good. I very much prefer honesty."

"I almost forgot!" I reach into my backpack and pull out the artichoke. She looks confused for a moment, but then I see her remember. She takes it from my hands.

"So can we kiss now?" I ask.

"Yes."

It's entirely different than it was on the street. Her mouth is still soft, but just as I relax into the kiss she bites my lower lip. I yelp in surprise, but I don't pull away. I can feel her smile. The bite is a warning. It's a *Don't think I've forgotten,* a *Don't you dare pull anything like that again.* And now her hand is on my neck, and she's pulling me even closer, and ohmy*god* we need to get out of here. But even though I know this is taking PDA one step too far, I can't stop kissing her. So we become the exhibit of us. One more spectacle in a museum packed with things to see. We breathe each other in. We tune the world out. Our kiss builds walls around us, until—

"Ah-hem!"

An elderly white-haired docent is standing a few feet from us, looking more amused than stern.

"Museum's closing," he says.

"I'm sorry!" I say, but the joy in my voice betrays how immensely far from sorry I am.

Violet takes my hand. She grins at the man.

"My girlfriend and I got carried away," she says, and he laughs, and we cross the tower to the elevator, and before the doors slide shut we're in each other's arms again.

SATURDAY

THURSDAY

FRIDAY

SATURDAY

MARK

21

We walked through the future and felt we were borrowing it.

Some of the people around us were famous. Some were only locally famous. None of them were teenagers.

But there we were, wandering through a mansion on Russian Hill, unclear whether we were playing a joke on them or they were playing a joke on us or if it was possible that none of this was a joke, that one day our lives would be like this, and at this moment we were getting an early glimpse, all because of a photographer I'd met at a club.

It was unclear who had money and who didn't. It was unclear who'd been invited and who'd crashed. It was unclear what we were celebrating, other than the celebratory fact that we'd made it here, that we were in this moment. The only person who seemed completely at home wasn't a person at all, but a cat named Renoir.

I looked around and saw the constellations, the multitude of versions of the kind of person a person could be. The alcohol and the lateness of the hour loosened people's tongues, loosened the music from their lips. I walked through it all, holding Katie's hand. We were Hansel and Gretel, and we had finally found the right house. The witches would let us lick the frosting from the bowl instead of hurling us into the oven.

"What are we doing here?" I asked her, again and again.

"We're taking it in," she replied. "We need to take it all in."

Inevitably, Ryan has to go to the bathroom, and Taylor and I are left alone together. He's brought over a DVD of the British version of *Queer as Folk* because he can't believe we've never seen it, even though, in fairness, it came out before we were born. It's paused during an act of tonguework that I hope Ryan's parents don't walk in and see. He hasn't talked to them yet, but is planning to this weekend. Earlier this evening, Taylor and I helped him strategize. At one point we role-played his parents. I got to be Mom.

All in all, the night's gone well, because after the coming-out conversation and role-play mostly we've been watching TV and snacking. In front of me, Ryan and Taylor haven't done anything more affectionate than lean against each other and touch arms.

I imagine it would be different if I weren't here. But I don't feel pressured to leave. Not by them. And not by myself.

I can do this. For my best friend.

Somehow as I'd been mentally preparing the whole day, the just-me-and-Taylor-in-a-room-together scenario was not one I'd pictured. I'm certainly not prepared for him to say thank you. Which is exactly what he does the minute Ryan's out of earshot.

"For what?" I ask.

He looks over, makes sure Ryan isn't coming back. "For being with him today," he says. "For helping him through this. For never forcing him out, which I know can't have been easy. My best friend came out two years after me, and it nearly drove me insane."

Of all the things that drove me insane, this was not the major one. But I don't tell Taylor that. Instead I say, "It was his choice. It was always his choice."

"I know. I'm just saying you're an awesome friend. You don't need me to tell you that at all. But just in case you ever doubt it, know that you are. I don't know Ryan all that well yet, but I do know *that*."

Go on! Shut up! Tell me more! Stop talking! My mind doesn't know what it wants from Taylor. The more he talks about me and Ryan being friends, the less I think he knows about us. I'm glad Ryan hasn't presented me to his new crush as a lovelorn burden. I'm glad our secrets are safe.

"I'm glad he found you," I say. "And if you ever hurt him, I will go for the proverbial kill."

Taylor nods. "I would expect no less."

Ryan returns and looks like he, too, hadn't planned on us being alone together.

"Don't worry—it went great," I tell him. Taylor smiles. I know I could tease right now—could pretend to have told Taylor something that Ryan wouldn't want him to know (like, say, our sexual history). But this is a big day. There's no room for teasing.

We go back to watching the show. The two of them cuddle closer. Ryan looks much more nervous with Taylor than he ever was with me. And he also looks much more comfortable with him than he ever was in front of anyone else with me.

This, I see, is the future.

"What are we doing here?" I asked Garrison Kline. We'd paid homage to his friends on their sofa perch. Now it was just him and the two of us. He still had his camera at the ready. His camera was always at the ready, as if something beautiful could happen at any moment.

He was checking in on me and Katie, our host even though this wasn't his party.

"We're going to make you the toast of the town," he told us. "You'd be surprised how easy that is."

"But why?" I couldn't comprehend. "Why do that for us?" Then I couldn't help myself. It was nagging at me too much, so I had to ask, "It's not because you want to sleep with me, is it?"

"Mark!" Katie said.

But Garrison Kline waved it off.

"No, it's a valid question. And it's good that you know to ask. Motives are important. And in this case, my motive is both simple and mysterious: I see something in you. And everyone—every single one of us—needs a little help on the way. I happen to be in a position where I can help. I was once on your side of the fence, and now I'm on this side."

"It's pretty nice on this side," Katie observed.

"It can be. On a good night."

"And this is how we become the toast of the town?" I asked. "Just by showing up? Having your friends spread the word?"

Garrison Kline shook his head. "No, it's more than that. I'll start with a simple question."

"Which is . . . ?"

"Who are you? Not your names—I know your names. But I need to know—*Who are you?*"

We all show up for the last day of school. Our lockers are mostly cleaned out. Classes are afterthoughts. The only reason we are here is to be with each other.

The last day of school has always seemed to me to be the doorway to summer—nothing further than that. But today it strikes me in a different way. I hear the future whispering that there will come a time when this building will not be my world. These kids will not be my life's sole population. There will come a day—soon—when I will walk away from this. Every now and then, I'll return as a ghost, as my memories step through these hallways. But I will already be in the after-life, which will be my new, better life.

I tell Katie how I'm feeling, and she seems to understand. I don't tell Ryan, because he has his own news to deal with. He's a one-man pride parade—last night the three of us decorated a shirt for him to wear. *By the way, I'm gay,* it says. A few people seem surprised when they read it.

But mostly?

People stop him to say how much they love the shirt.

* * *

Who are you?

Kate answered Garrison Kline instantly.

"I'm an artist."

He smiled. "I don't doubt it. But show me some proof."

So she took out her phone, looking as nervous as I must have looked when I'd stepped onto that bar in my underwear. She showed him some photos of her work. He seemed genuinely impressed.

"This has suddenly become much more interesting," he said once he'd swiped through. Then he turned to me. "How about you? Who are you?"

And because I was still hurt, and because I was still aware of the silence of the phone in my pocket, I found myself saying, "I'm not Ryan's boyfriend."

"I'm not sure I understand."

"Neither do I."

Garrison Kline nodded. Then, gently, he said, "I don't think that's a good answer, because I don't think that's an accurate answer. I want you to try again. Who are you?"

"I am becoming—" I started. Then I tried again. "I am becoming—"

But I couldn't figure out the end of the sentence.

"Maybe that's your answer," Katie said. "You're becoming. You're in the process of becoming. You just don't know what yet."

That felt right. It felt okay to stop there, for now, as we walked through the future.

Satisfied, the photographer began to take our picture. Solo and together.

It was only the next morning that we would see:

We looked great.

* * *

I am walking on my own to Pink Saturday. Tomorrow Ryan and Taylor and some of Taylor's friends will join us for the parade, but today it's only me who's meeting up with Katie and her contingent.

It's only as I'm a block away from the Castro that I realize: I've done this all myself. This is the first time I've ever come here on my own, and the remarkable thing is that I'm only noticing it now. I take my place in the crowd—a crowd that doesn't feel anonymous, because each of us is so individual. There are too many types of us to be counted; there are too many variations of our pride to be pigeonholed. I see people my age and people five times my age. I see all of these people freed from their given definitions and fashioning their own way of being defined. I get looks from guys, for sure—and while I don't shy away from them, I don't fall into them, either. I am not here to pick up or be picked up. I am here to be with my friends.

From the top of Castro Street, it looks like a river of people. It looks, I realize, like a march—rows and rows of people, gathered to exert their power. Only this time we aren't marching. We don't need to show our numbers to show our worth. This time our power comes from staying in this space, from walking the hallowed ground of our history and bringing it to life. I am alone, yes. But I am a part of this. I am a part of everything. I feel it—I've been living in a world, but what I have is a universe.

Katie texts to say she's waiting under the Castro Theatre's neon marquee. Without another thought—without any hesitation—I plunge in and head toward her. I join the fray.

I'm ready now.

I am becoming—

Kate

22

"You're here!" I shout when I see him.

Mark has broken free of the crowd. He's looking at me and grinning, and I grab him in a hug.

"It's just you," he says. "And, oh my *God*, look at you!"

I laugh. This morning I raided my art supplies and the costume bin in the garage. I arrived at Lehna's house with a bag full of paints and body glitter, tutus and ribbons and everything rainbow I could find, relics from our pride-filled freshman year.

She had already assembled her outfit carefully. A backwards cap, shorts, and a crop-top shirt with the sleeves cut off. I talked her into adding rainbow suspenders, and then she told me all about Candace as I assembled my outfit.

I settled on the same jeans I wore last Saturday, but this

time with a metallic gold leotard and a pair of white angel wings. I let my hair fall down past my shoulders, and I dabbed gold glitter on my cheeks and then I painted my arms in so many shades of pink and red and gold, all swirls and stars and joy.

Mark says, "You look like a lesbian artist fairy."

And I laugh again because he looks so much like himself in his jeans and plain T-shirt and baseball cap from our school team. And by that, I mean he looks perfect. So far from a boy trying to win the love of his best friend by dancing almost naked on a bar. So far from someone too heartbroken to get out of bed. So far from a boy waiting for me, lost, on a sidewalk.

I hug him again.

"They're expecting us back in half an hour," I say. "That's when Violet gets here."

"Thirty minutes of our own," he says. "What should we fill them with?"

I grab his hand and pull him back into the crowd.

"Where are we going?" he asks, but I don't answer him until we're at the entrance of Happy Happy and he laughs and says, "Perfect," and I say, "I thought so, too."

A minute later we're carrying gin and tonics to the table where I sat when this all started. The bar itself is almost quiet. The true party is out on the street; most of the bars won't fill until later. There's too much to see, and there's the need to be seen. But for now all I want are a few minutes with my friend. I've already heard about his day with Taylor and Ryan. He already knows how excited I am about seeing Violet.

Mark lifts his glass.

"We need to toast," he says.

"Yes."

"What a week," he says.

"Somehow we survived it."

"We more than survived it. We kicked this week's ass."

"We tongue kissed it."

"We fucking *married* it," Mark says. "This week will be with us forever."

We clink glasses, take sips, and it's the weakest gin and tonic I've ever had, but I don't mind.

"I think he knows we're underage," Mark whispers.

We grin at each other, and I will be happy if all we do is sit and sip our tonic waters in the presence of each other for the rest of our minutes alone, but then the door opens and fills the bar with the roar of the street. We turn to look and our mouths drop in synchronized disbelief.

Here's another teenager, younger than us. He squints and then sees us. He freezes and steps back toward the door. I gesture him over.

"Should I try to get a drink?" he says once he's reached us. And then, whispering, *"I don't have a fake ID."*

Even as he's saying it, he's looking through his wallet as though an ID may magically appear.

"Not worth it," I say. "This is a monumental waste of ten dollars."

He puts his wallet in his pocket, but then he has nothing to do with his hands, and I see that they're shaking.

"What are you doing here?" Mark asks him.

"Oh, uh," the boy stammers. "I, um . . . I was just . . ."

If Garrison Kline were here, he'd take a look at this boy and know exactly the right thing to say. He wouldn't look into the boy's soul, but he'd make him look into it himself, until what he saw didn't scare him so much anymore.

But Garrison Kline has disappeared from our lives in a puff of fairy godfather smoke. Somehow, I can feel that with certainty. All we have, at least for now, are ourselves and each other.

We introduce ourselves, and the kid says his name is Wyatt and that he read about the bar on the Internet and that it seemed like kind of a cool place to just, you know, check out sometime, and he has no idea why he's even here, he just felt like getting out of the house, and I can't listen to him talk like this anymore.

On his shirt is a tiny rainbow pin. I touch it.

"This is beautiful," I say, even though it's only flimsy metal and cheap paint. "Did you get it for today?"

He stops his rambling. He nods.

"Someone handed it to me when I got off BART."

"And how does it feel to wear it?"

He breathes in and exhales. Smiles at the table and wipes his forehead with his arm.

He gathers the courage and looks at me.

"Feels good," he says.

"Happy first Pride, Wyatt," I say solemnly.

"Thanks," he says.

Hiding and denying and being afraid is no way to treat love. Love demands bravery. No matter the occasion, love expects us to rise, and with that in mind I check my phone.

"Boys," I say. "We have a party to attend."

The party has spilled from Shelbie's house to the street, where some neighbors are blasting music from a huge speaker in their garage. Lehna and Candace are sitting with their arms around each other on Shelbie's stoop. Lehna smiles when she sees me. June and Uma are dancing along with so many others. I don't know if the people around them are Shelbie's friends, but I *do* know that on a day like today there is no such thing as a stranger.

"Let's dance," I say to the boys.

"I've never danced with a girl in a leotard and wings before," Wyatt says.

"I bet you've never danced with a guy before, either," Mark says, and Wyatt blushes, and Mark grabs his hand.

The warm sun. The people filling the streets. The bass so powerful it thrums through me. The people hawking Jell-O shots and bottles of water. The drag queens and drag kings. The trans men and trans women. The straight couples cheering us on. The topless girls, waving from apartments above us. The gay boys on fire escapes, shaking their asses. The bears, holding hands in matching wedding rings. The lesbian moms with toddlers on their shoulders. And those not as easily identified or defined. The bi, the genderqueer, the questioning. All of us with love in our hearts.

We are all a part of this.

My phone vibrates.

Walking through Dolores Park. Found Greer and Quinn! Meet us here?

"Dolores Park?" I call out, and Shelbie runs inside and returns with a picnic blanket. We push through the crowds together.

On Dolores Street, the line of motorcycles and scooters stretches for blocks, topped by women of all ages and colors, wearing spike heels and combat boots, lingerie, and leather, and in one case nothing at all. The sun is warm on my skin and the paint on my arms is still bright. I catch a glimpse of myself in the rearview mirror of a car and my cheeks still sparkle gold.

Violet, I think.

Her name isn't a spell I'm trying to cast or a way to forget anymore. It's a thrill that courses through me, a current of love, and then there she is, waving.

"You look *incredible*," she says, and she touches my cheeks, and she touches my hair, and the neckline of the leotard, and the edges of the wings. She spins me around and then she wraps her arms around my neck and she's kissing me here, under the hot sun, her mouth warm and soft, and I can't get enough of her.

We kiss, and kiss, and kiss.

I will never get enough of her.

And when we stop kissing, I say, "I have something to tell you."

"Tell me."

"My parents agreed," I say. "I sent an email to the admissions office. So it's official: I'm free for another year."

"Oh, Kate," she says. "Let's do something amazing."

The motorcycles roar to life. The pigeons take flight. The crowd goes wild.

Quinn's dressed in a bright pink bunny suit.

"It looks hot in there!" I shout over the revving engines.

"Say that again?" he yells back.

"I said, it looks hot in there!"

"That's what I thought you said!"

And then, with a flourish, he unzips the suit and steps out of it in only a pink sparkly Speedo.

"Oh, God," I say. "Have you been waiting all day to do that?"

"Yes," he says, and starts dancing.

And the sun rises higher in the sky and then begins its descent. We take up three tables in a crowded Mexican restaurant and sit next to someone else every time someone yells, "Switch!" We carry our plates and silverware to new chairs and ignore the annoyance of our frenzied waiters.

I sit next to Violet and hold her hand.

I sit next to Wyatt and dab glitter on his cheekbones.

I sit next to Lehna and make dinner plans for after graduation.

I sit next to Greer and tell them I loved their poem.

I sit next to Mark and say, "Let's know each other like this for a very long time."

I sit next to Quinn, who plants a kiss on my mouth for old times' sake.

I sit next to a kid I don't know. "What's your name?" I ask. "Sky," she says.

I sit next to Violet again. She says, "We could drive across country. We could volunteer to build houses. We could go live on a farm. I'm still thinking."

We join yet another street dance party. We are swept into a stranger's living room to judge a round of drunken karaoke. We stand in line at Bi-Rite for ice cream and end up back at the park with sticky hands, trying to predict who we'll all be in five years.

Shelbie says we can stay over at her place tonight, be among the first to show up for the parade tomorrow. Everyone texts their parents—except Greer, who calls the shelter—and all the parents and Greer's guardian say yes. Tomorrow we will line up along Market Street, shoulder to shoulder. The Dykes on Bikes will be back to kick everything off, and the mayor will be there, and all of the gay cops and firefighters. The Sisters of Perpetual Indulgence will be in full drag, lip-synching to some Katy Perry song. There will be floats and classic cars, and chants and songs and tears. There will be old people who fought hard for what we all have now. There will be babies who will only know a country where everyone can marry. There will be signs reminding us of how far we still have to go. We'll watch everyone go by, and our hearts will swell with the sight of it.

But not yet.

It's late now, and we're all walking to Walgreens for toothbrushes and a couple extra pillows. It's late, but we're still wide awake, and each time Violet touches me I'm filled with wonder, because soon we'll be finding a quiet patch of floor in Shelbie's living room to share all night.

"Okay, three more," she says. "We could go to the Grand Canyon. We could teach ourselves to cook. We could learn a dying language and keep it alive."

"How will we choose?"

"We'll just pick something," she says. "It doesn't even matter what."

We've gotten a few steps ahead of the group. I slow down, turn to see them. We're on our own now, on an empty street, but the sounds of celebration echo through the night. And here we are. Lehna and Candace and Shelbie, June and Uma, Mark and Quinn and Wyatt and Sky and Greer, and Violet, and me. I don't know if we'll all ever be together like this again. I don't know if Sky and Wyatt and Greer will become my friends for life or only for these two short days. I don't know if Lehna and I will end up sitting on a porch together, bickering in our old age, or if this week will have been the beginning of a slow fade from each other's lives. I don't know if Violet and I will make it . . . but I hope so, I hope so. They've all caught up now, at the corner of this street, with the glow of the drugstore only a block in the distance. And we step off the curb, all of us together, as if to say, Here we come—through hard days and good ones, through despair and through exhilaration, in love and out of love, for just now or for forever. Here we come. It's our parade.

ACKNOWLEDGMENTS

This book first started during a conversation on October 11, 2012, and the first chapter of it was sent on January 20, 2013, starting a back-and-forth pattern that would finish on June 28, 2015. It is safe to say that neither of us in October 2012 imagined that the hypothetical book we were talking about would be completed the weekend of (a) Pride Week when we were both (b) in San Francisco right after (c) the Supreme Court ruled in favor of marriage rights for people like us. We liked to imagine Katie and Mark celebrating along with us in the streets.

There are many people we have to thank for the book you have in your hands. Together, we would like to thank the extraordinary Sara Goodman, whose infectious excitement and thoughtful words have always been deeply appreciated. We'd also like to thank everyone else at St. Martin's, and at all of our foreign publishers, for believing in this book. Our agents, Sara Crowe and Bill Clegg, and the many people who support them, are also the beneficiaries of our profound gratitude.

Nina would like to thank the teenagers she's known, whether in life or by way of a laptop screen, who have been unafraid to voice their uncertainty. You've reminded her that it can be a gift to not have it all figured out. She'd also like to thank a certain blond girl who, in 2010 English Comp, said she was afraid she would stop dancing when she grew up and forget that it had once been everything to her. Finally, many thanks to her writing group for their moral and artistic support and her friends and family for making her world a beautiful place, especially Amanda, for giving her time to write so many of these chapters, and Kristyn and Juliet, for innumerable daily wonders.

David would like to thank his family and friends (as always), with special shout-outs to Stephanie Perkins, Rainbow Rowell, and all of the Openly YA authors he's toured with over the past few years, including (but not at all limited to) Bill Konigsberg, Sandy London, Aaron Hartzler, Sara Farizan, Will Walton, Adam Silvera, and Juno Dawson. He'd also like to thank Nancy Garden, for leading the way for all the rest of us, and Jen Corn, Sarah (Roo) Cline, their kids Maizie and Amon, Jane Mason, Sarah Hines Stephens, and everyone at Books Inc., because I couldn't imagine writing a San Francisco book without tipping my hat to you.

And from both of us—thank you to the readers who keep us going, time and time again.